The Last Twist of the Knife

T0151776

João Almino

THE LAST TWIST
OF THE KNIFE

Translated from the Portuguese by Elizabeth Lowe

DALKEY ARCHIVE PRESS
Dallas / Dublin

Originally published in Portuguese by Editora Record as *Entre facas, algodão* in 2017.

Copyright © 2017 by João Almino.

Translation copyright © 2021 by Elizabeth Lowe.

First Dalkey Archive edition, 2021.

CIP Data available upon request.

Dalkey Archive Press
Dallas / Dublin

Work published with the support of the Brazilian Ministry of Culture / National Library Foundation
Obra publicada com o apoio do Ministério da Cultura do Brasil / Fundação Biblioteca Nacional

MINISTÉRIO DA CULTURA
Fundação BIBLIOTECA NACIONAL

Printed on permanent/durable acid-free paper.
www.dalkeyarchive.com

I thank my wife, Bia Wouk, for her careful reading, and Natália Almino Gondim for her suggestions.

In memory of Maria José Almino de Queiroz, Natália de Queiroz e Souza and João Almino de Souza

Car aux troubles de la mémoire sont liées les intermittences du cœur.

Marcel Proust

The lamp said,
"Four o'clock,
Here is the number on the door.
Memory!
You have the key,
The little lamp spreads a ring on the stair,
Mount.
The bed is open; the toothbrush hangs on the wall,
Put your shoes at the door, sleep, prepare for life."

The last twist of the knife.

T.S. Eliot

Contents

The Last Twist of the Knife

1. Taguaatinga, Sector A North, QNA 32

March 31

CLARICE HAD SENT a message on Facebook.

"What does she want from you?" Patrícia asked me, more bitterly than ever. We were sitting on a sofa in the living room.

Rain was coming down in torrents.

"You read it. You know as much as I do."

I had forgotten to log out of Facebook. Patrícia had used this as an opportunity to scroll through my messages. Unacceptable.

"No, no I didn't read it. I just saw she had messaged you."

"Right. You must have seen she doesn't want anything from me. She just gave me a tip."

"About what?"

What a pain! Patrícia wants to control me. I could have told her the truth, if she didn't already know it. It didn't matter to me. Clarice's message wasn't personal. There was nothing to indicate there was any affection

between us. Absolutely nothing! It was almost busi-
ness-like. She had learned from my friend Arnaldo about
my interest in buying land in that area and she let me
know about a property for sale. She also gave me her
e-mail address and cell number. Just that.

"It's not important," I answered.

"It is too. Do you think I've forgotten your history
with that bitch?"

Gratuitous aggression. How I regretted having told
her everything about my past. Giving her details about
Clarice, of all people. I really am an idiot, an imbecile!

Or rather, I was. That was in the very beginning, when
we thought that since we were in love and the world
wouldn't make sense if we weren't together, we had to
open our hearts and tell each other everything, absolutely everything. Total sincerity. Respect for the truth.
It couldn't be hidden. Patrícia never forgot the slightest
detail about Clarice.

It was still raining. Lightning lit up the windows.
The thunder rumbled without stopping, adding drama
to our discussion.

"It doesn't mean shit. The place is for sale, yes. It's
what I want. What I want, understand? It's the place
where I spent my childhood."

In her message Clarice says that my house was
destroyed. But the lot for sale still has the old big house
from her father's ranch, Black Creek. What memories
Black Creek brings back to me! If she didn't read it,
Patrícia guessed what the message said, because she asked:

"And why doesn't she buy it?"

Irritated, I answered, "because she wants me to buy it."

"Oh, so that's it! The bitch wants you to live next door to her."

How did she know that Clarice lived near the property? Her message didn't say that. The truth is, if I buy the land, I'll practically be Clarice's neighbor.

"No. I want to live near her. I want to, understand?" I answered sarcastically, raising my voice.

"May I ask why? You don't need to answer, I get it," she said, without acknowledging my sarcasm.

In fact, I wasn't being sarcastic. It would give me enormous pleasure to be Clarice's neighbor.

"Just because," I answered.

"So buy that crappy piece of land and bury yourself on it," Patrícia yelled. "Get out, you piece of shit. I knew I couldn't trust you!"

My marriage to Patrícia had survived infidelities and such a stupid matter shouldn't have made her so mad.

"Fine, that's what I'll do," I said impulsively, because one provocation leads to another and then another.

"Asshole! Get out of this house," she shouted even more loudly. The harangue went on for hours, with insane screaming. It further eroded our ever-weakening marriage. Suffice it to say that without heed to the rain, Patrícia started throwing my clothes out the window. A shoe landed on the sidewalk on the other side of the street and filled up with rainwater.

I didn't give in. In the rain, I gathered my things, not caring how ridiculous I looked to the neighbors, and went back into the house. Patrícia tried to attack me physically. I just defended myself; I didn't want to be arrested. Then I locked myself in a bedroom. I decided I would leave, but I wouldn't let myself be evicted. Patrícia didn't push it any further. She stopped speaking to me, and I followed suit. If she didn't kick me out, then I'd land on my feet.

April 1

I'm not kidding, despite it being April Fools' Day. If I take a good look, my marriage with Patrícia isn't among the worst. We have a lot in common. We used to talk, which not every couple can say. We kissed each other, a noteworthy feat after decades of marriage. And Patrícia's jealousy is proof that she still loves me.

I don't feel the same jealousy as she does, because she stopped singing in bars a long time ago, and today I don't see a worthy rival in any of her colleagues at the Post Office. I didn't have the least intention of separating from her. But the fight swelled like a soufflé and got out of my control. We've gone beyond the point of repairing our relationship. It makes me think it's really best for me to return to the Northeast.

I'm going to answer Clarice. I'll ask for details about the person selling the land. If I can negotiate a good price, I'll ask if she will agree to my giving her a power of attorney so she can act as my proxy at the closing in the registry in Várzea Pacífica.

April, Easter

Clarice gave me the seller's number. After negotiating the terms of the purchase, I called her cellphone. I thought it best to talk. She agreed to the power of attorney. We didn't touch on the more personal matter. I asked about Miguel, her brother. He's fine, except for his business difficulties. He spends most of his time on the road.

I thought of so many things before calling her . . . I wanted to ask if she remembered this or that moment, how she feels living alone on a ranch, if she ever thought about me . . . I stifled the impulse. But it was possible to sense the emotion in her voice. I paid special attention to what she said:

"It's so good that you're coming back."

If I dig deep, I find many memories of her. Dreams have a memory. The Clarice of the future—I think she exists, despite everything—has much of the Clarice of the past.

If I'm not mistaken it was in fifty-eight, during the worst of the drought, when for the first time I felt something like love for her. I don't want to say too much because I'm not sure and I can't remember it very well. I was very young. It might have been that year or some other year that the litany of sounds was the same, bats flying at dawn, trees stripped of their leaves, green only in the juazeiro tree, in the *xique-xique* and *mandacarú* cactus, animal carcasses along the dusty roads that exhaled their hot breath, the sun burning and drying up the world, and drying me up inside. In short, the same desolation, now traveled by some tanker truck and waiting for the Francisco River transposition.

Or maybe it had been winter, because I remember water in the reservoir, the shiny light green of the thorny squat trees, the green field behind the reservoir, and I woke up early to go to the barn to milk the cows. I'm not sure, and I apologize to anyone reading this. Or, forget that, I won't apologize, because I shouldn't have to ask to be forgiven for my contradictions if they are the very contradictions of the backlands, dry or wet, contradictions that still exist today. When it's dry, the landscape is gray, marked with boulders and skulls; I'm not exaggerating. When it's wet, too wet, it frightens people and causes disasters.

April 21
It's a holiday and I stayed at home. I thought that Patrícia would want to upset me. She has ignored me, at least until now. I'm free to continue these notes about my times in Black Creek, Várzea Pacífica, back when Clarice was so important to me. One day, who knows, I'll show these pages to her.

It may be that I don't even remember correctly. It may be that the reality of that past exists only in my imagination. I must be mixing up several droughts and several floods. So, yes, I must apologize for this confusion to anyone who happens to read these notes, written quickly and without regard for style or vocabulary.

I look at my past not with pride, but with resignation.

Much of the turbulence that tormented me has subsided. What aroused passion in me is now filed in my memory like photographs in an album with pages yellowed by time. Some of the photos are covered in mold. Others are so stuck together that when you try to peel them apart, they tear, leaving white gashes.

Clarice is the exception. My memory of her is as clear as a photograph kept with care in the bottom of one of my drawers. In it she looks at me with an expression that I feel is one of love, and which even today sends quivers through my body.

I recover pieces of myself to create this contradictory and true story that torments me. That's why I have to share it. It is as contradictory and true as the backlands; my mother punished me and protected me, and my godfather, Clarice's father, was severe and affectionate. I accepted their mood changes the same way I accepted the mood changes of nature. I thought my joys and sorrows were normal.

In winter, rain covered the green land, our boots trampled mud over the floor, the conversation and laughter lingered on the porch of the big house of my godparents, the songs of the cowboys rose up from the pastures, the mosquitos bit me in our red brick house. I'd roll myself up in the hammock, cover myself with the sheet, leaving just my nose exposed, and listen to the raindrops on the roof.

At the height of the drought, the merciless sun punished Black Creek Ranch and blinded me. The dust whipped the gray fields, with its bare trees, dazed people stewing with irritation in the heat, the wells were dry, the reservoir and the barn were empty, the cattle had migrated to Piauí.

Here again I might be mixing up time periods. Forgive me. I may be conflating the drought of one year with the prolonged summer of another. But I'm not inventing anything; at most it's my memory that betrays me here and there. It's my age; at seventy your memory falters. What is true is that the landscapes of the drought always display the same calcified trees, the same ashen ruins and the same irritation. I think that above all it is the landscapes of the drought that brand backlands people like me.

May 1

I visit here on holidays, I don't even know why. Today I imagine there are speeches and protests. I prefer to concentrate on my notes. I've dug deep for my oldest memories.

There must be others, but the ones that came to me first were from that day when I was six, propped up against a corner of the porch balustrade of the big house of my godfather, Clarice's father, I was listening to the Hitachi battery powered radio, a novelty freshly arrived in Black Creek, which livened up the verandah with *forró* music interrupted by squeals due to the bad transmission. The radio battery was charged by a wind turbine, now disconnected. In another corner of the balustrade sat Clarice's grandmother, Dona Leopolda, fat, round-faced and jowly, wearing a floral dress to mid-calf. She was making cigars, cutting the strings of tobacco with a sharp knife as she puffed on a pipe, blowing smoke rings. An empty white hammock swung on the porch, rocked by a strong northeast wind. From the porch you could see a room that was separate from the house, and through the doors, saddles and halters, lengths of stretched leather, barrels on the floor, and vests hanging on hammock hooks. Perhaps it is my memory of one day. Or perhaps, more likely, of many days that repeated themselves exactly, without adding or taking away anything.

Arnaldo, a black boy, who was blacker and two years older than I, and who also lives close to the little ranch I want to buy and with whom I've already been in touch, called me to go to the reservoir and fetch water. He lived with his father, Mr. Rodolfo, and his mother, Miss Vitória, and a throng of brothers and sisters, on the neighboring farm, owned by my godfather's brother, whom I called "Uncle." We went with Quinquim, whose belly was bloated with parasites, but who was thin everywhere else; he was the color of spoiled milk and mentally retarded; he lolled his tongue and had just two friends: me and the donkey Gray. Gray knew the way to the reservoir, he went first. Every day he carried the water. Sometimes he came back on his own, he didn't need people, and he would wait for us to unload the jugs.

I considered Arnaldo to be my superior, and with reason. He knew the names of all the livestock—cows and calves—he knew how to help Quinquim with the

water jugs and he filled the four clay barrels that rested
on a wood platform in the shed next to the big house—
Arnaldo tells me they've now been replaced by the cistern. Next to them we placed strings of garlic, onions,
clay cooking pots, and bags of salt. Early in the morning
we would bring in the cans of milk, which in a corner
of the kitchen were to be turned into fresh curd cheese
or *coalhada*. We brought in the bunches of bananas—
baba-de-boi bananas, tiny "apple" bananas, silver and
green bananas—which as they ripened exhaled their
aroma. My godfather, Clarice's father, said to put the
green bananas next to the ripest ones so they would
ripen more quickly. Arnaldo and I sometimes stole silver
bananas when they started to turn yellow and we'd eat
them while we walked down to the reservoir with Gray.

There are things, as I've already said, that I don't quite
remember; I'm sorry. I don't know if it was that day
or some other day when the mute who lived on the
ranch of Clarice's uncle, whom I called "Uncle," bathed
naked in the reservoir. Since she was deaf, she didn't
hear the noise of our footsteps, mine and Arnaldo's. If
she saw us, she pretended she didn't, and we pretended
not to believe that she was pretending. It wasn't the first
time. Even though we made fun of her when she made
faces and incomprehensible noises with her tongue, she
was the main attraction of the walk. We told Miguel,
Clarice's brother, exaggerating the beauty of her thighs,
her buttocks and her breasts, and he was mad with envy.
But we couldn't truthfully say that her face was pretty,
even though her long, blond, straight hair fell over her

shoulders beautifully, because, this we agreed, the ugliness of her face frightened us.

May 2

One day I made a bet with Arnaldo on our run—a special day for one simple reason: it had to do with Clarice, about whom, after all, I wanted to talk. Arnaldo ran faster than I did. I felt defeated. I fell and scraped my knees. It was the end of the world. Or rather its beginning.

The glaring sun lit us up with yellow shapes. It projected the pillars of the verandah onto the big house, streaking the floor and clay pots with black, violent shadows. That day has stayed with me until now, with a feeling of drama and hope.

The drama: that the coming nightfall would deprive me of its protective mantle; that I would always trip over the stones on the hillside; that the horizon would always be uncertain; that, lost, I wouldn't find my way.

The hope: that someone would save me from disaster. From the top of the hill, having scraped my knees on the stones, seeing the blood, I also saw the big house and, in front of it, Clarice, who was coming to help me.

A squawking guinea fowl was flying around the yard afraid of the leather-clad cowhands. Then a band of gypsies appeared, visitors that passed through every two or three months, leading packs of mules and horses loaded with goods for sale. They assembled under the tamarind tree in the yard.

"Are you selling this horse? Where is its brand?" asked Clarice's father, his angry voice high-pitched, focusing on a small detail, suspicious of the gypsies and ignoring my bloody knees.

I didn't have any money and I wanted to buy a present for Clarice. With gestures, one of the gypsies gave me to understand that I could pay later. I picked a gold ring set with a stone, certainly fake, which I gave Clarice as a present when the sun was already hiding away, ashamed, and the chickens were quieting down in the roost.

At night—it might have been that day or if it wasn't, then I've mixed it up with another day, a natural extension of that one—there was an enormous bonfire, made of many cartloads of firewood, in front of the big house. It must have been June, maybe even the twenty-fourth, the feast of St. John, who knows? The flames illuminated the smiling faces, sometimes open-mouthed with loud laughter, the people circling the fire, the roasting green corn. On the verandah, the game was different, a serious one: I scattered drops from a melting candle on the floor and the wax formed a letter C, C for Clarice. Happiness.

Those days there was talk of young women being kidnapped by men who wanted to marry them, and that one such abduction had taken place in Várzea Pacífica. The boy would take the girl and the families would be forced to hold a wedding. I imagined arriving on horseback at one of the windows of the big house and lifting Clarice up on to the saddle. Would she go for it?

Today I talked with Arnaldo. We haven't seen each other in years, but every time we talk it's as if we saw each other only yesterday. Let's communicate through WhatsApp, he suggested. A guy he knows is selling a used car. I'm selling mine here in Taguatinga to buy this other one when I get to Várzea Pacífica if it's still for sale. I won't buy it sight unseen.

I'm going to introduce a technique to the farm for direct cotton planting with the introduction of rotating crops. I've already looked into a list of solar energy companies in the Fortaleza region since I'm going to install solar energy panels, at least for the needs of the main house, which won't be the big house, but my own modern, comfortable house. And I'll upgrade the precarious irrigation system, that is years old. What's new is there are two artesian wells on the property and the house already has a cistern, so Arnaldo tells me.

May 7
When I think of the upcoming trip to Black Creek, the past takes on a gray cast, vague and out of focus. Here and there are lights that illuminate it, tears in the dark and without continuity: the wrinkled face of my grandmother, my mother's chintz dresses, the white jacket and shiny boots of my godfather, Clarice's father, the bells swaying on the necks of the milk cows when they go out to pasture early in the morning and on their return to the barn in the afternoon, the top that I played with on the cement sidewalk of the big house, the parrots flying

when the hot northwest wind arrived, stirring the dry branches, my little white lamb that I rode before taking it to the pen in the late afternoon, the vest, chaps, breastplate and leather hat of Mr. Rodolfo, father of my friend Arnaldo and husband of the lovely Vitória.

Vitória . . . should I also talk about her? I remember that in the window of her poor house, she would give me a mysterious smile with her perfectly straight teeth, wearing a light dress with a neckline that showed the crease between her breasts. No, no I won't talk about her. It's just a passing image, a smile in a window, a boy's desire.

Looking at the ashes of the past, I see callused hands on the handle of the spade and others, delicate, Clarice's, caressing my chickenpox blisters, which she wanted to pop. I see the cotton fields, white, very white, the hills rising and falling into the distance and Arnaldo calling me to hunt doves. I'd keep him company while he did his chores, always riding the donkey. And then I hear his complicit laughter on the way, harsh voices giving me orders, others warming me.

Suddenly my sister Zuleida appears. Today, she lives in Recife. She is two years older than I am and she used to scold me over some prank and I'd never understand why and still don't today. Pieces of the past arrive that either frighten me or invite me to a reunion. It's what I see, what I hear. The rest I imagine; should I describe it?

I close my eyes. In the distance appears the landscape of the reservoir, the brightness punctuated by ducks and herons. Are they still there? Sometimes I would go down with Arnaldo, leading the donkey to the water's edge to graze on grass, melons, or squash. The melons were spread like weeds, a green carpet in the middle of the corn fields. We'd fill the jugs and Gray would strain to climb the rocky hill so that we could deposit the cargo in the barrels in the storehouse next to the big house.

May 21
My father doesn't appear in these shafts of light that I see through the drawn curtains of the past. I lie. He appears, a lot, when I see, astonished, what I didn't see then: the knife tearing open his belly, the blood flowing like a river along the ground, the corpse propped against a door in an alley of Várzea Pacífica, the little town near the ranch at Black Creek where we lived . . .

And then perhaps what I saw at the age of just two, I'm not sure, the images are out of focus: a deep grave, a mound of dirt with flowers and a cross . . . He's in a terrible story that torments me always. Or else he's in a photograph with mother, a photograph touched up with color, in which mother's black face is pink and her lips are covered with a red lipstick I never saw her wear in real life. A framed photograph hanging on the wall of our poor house of red brick.

Father's assassin roils something inside me, something that will explode, I'm certain. Revenge? When I get to Black Creek and above all when I visit Várzea Pacífica, I will still face this fact of the past that doesn't stop tormenting me. I will have to face the assassin.

I leave in a week's time, everything is arranged. I flee from the coming drought. Not a drop of water has fallen on this plateau.

Clarice sent me the deed of the land I bought by proxy. I packed my things and exactly thirteen days ago I shipped a small container of goods that Arnaldo will receive and arrange in the ranch house. I also asked him to buy cotton seeds to plant when I arrive.

Still May 21
Of course I don't remember Daddy's death the way I remember my grandmother's, his mother, the first dying person I saw close up. She couldn't eat or drink. When she was thirsty, they would moisten her lips. She was just skin and bones, her expression one of suffering and goodness. She lived with us—with Mama, my sister Zuleide, and me—in the back of our red brick house. I learned years later that my grandfather, a jealous man, mistreated her. He would forbid her to leave the house. Because of a few stares in church, he gave her such a bad beating that it left permanent marks on her body. As far as I know, she never complained of this.

On her death bed, she wanted me to be at her side. A coward, I fled. I got tired of staying with her and I abandoned her. I did not forgive myself when, on awakening, I saw her body lying with cotton wads in her nostrils.

At the funeral I held on to Mama's skirt. She was one of the pallbearers, the only woman, the others were all men. I did not see the coffin being lowered into the ground. With a stick from a tree branch I went hunting for a lizard. That's how I react to big events, tragedies, by seeking something at the margins to save me, something to distract me, but to this day I am hounded by guilt for this. Could it be that I write to redeem myself of my guilt?

They bought me black Nycron pants that didn't wrinkle and they pinned a black ribbon on the pocket of my white cotton shirt. Mama wore black for six months and for another six she wore black and white. That's what I remember and perhaps that is all that is left to me of my grandmother's death.

My mother also died years ago, a terrible death caused by a transfusion of AIDS-infected blood. At the time I was living in Taguatinga, and she was still in Mondubim, on the outskirts of Fortaleza, where I had kept her company for a few years. I went to see her. I lay down on her bed, held her hand, tried to calm her; she would overcome the illness, I lied. She did not know it was AIDS, the doctors had told her only that it was a strange and terrible virus against which they had given her experimental injections. Hiding from her, I had the biggest cry of my life. She died the day I had to return to Taguatinga. She did not pass into eternal life, the way they told me. Death is what is eternal. It doesn't do any good to say that in nature everything renews itself. Mama could never come back.

I shall close my funeral commentary by saying that my godfather, Clarice's father, died of disappointment more than of cancer, at the age of eighty. He had the best treatment in a hospital in São Paulo, where they took him when his cancer metastasized. I paid him a visit in the hospital. He got emotional when he saw me; he was as sweet as ever.

At his request, the body was cremated and the ashes were thrown into Black Creek, the creek that gives its name to the ranch and will now give its name to my property, which is much smaller than the old Black Creek, I must confess.

When my godfather died, I talked with Clarice over the phone. She told me that she had not thrown all of his ashes into the creek. She had kept the equivalent of a teaspoon in a little metal box, which I never saw.

May 22
At Black Creek, my godfather made his living from cotton farming and the cultivation of *oiticica* and *carnaúba* palms. His income came mostly from cotton. I remember that he would proudly pull apart the cotton boll to display the length of the fiber. He sold the *oiticica* and *carnaúba* seeds to intermediaries that in turn sent them south and overseas. A part of the seeds went into the cattle feed.

He was an industrial entrepreneur, the kind of figure who previously hadn't existed in the backlands. In a factory in Várzea Pacífica, the only one in the region, which today is run by his son Miguel, my best friend from childhood, they manufactured meal in milled or compacted form, and cotton oil. Attentive to prices on the international market, he would send the unprocessed cotton to Fortaleza, from where it was exported.

The harvests were never the same. I learned from Miguel that in 1976 and 1977 the plantation had its best yield, and that in 1982 and 1983 there was a boll-weevil plague that caused terrible damage. Since 2000, and especially in 2002, it has been a disaster: meager harvests, despite investments to replace arboreal with herbaceous cotton, which has shorter fibers, but is more productive. It was impossible to compete with imported cotton and what was being produced in São Paulo and Mato Grosso.

From what they told me, even before I was born my godfather took care not only of his family, but ours as well. Or rather, he protected Daddy, whom he employed in the Várzea Pacífica factory, at the time when Mama was pregnant with my sister Zuleide. After Daddy was murdered, he sheltered all of us at the Black Creek ranch and treated me like a son. He had an oval face, a broad forehead, and always a smile on his thin lips. His fits of anger were rare. Perhaps because he was a sweet man, and soft-spoken, they presumed that he was controlled by his wife and called him white belly.

For her, the woman who called herself my godmother, I never had warm feelings. Her hair was as bushy as the savage brush, her mouth was wrinkled, and evil shone in her big predatory eyes, which her tortoise-shell glasses could not conceal. She would scold me for nothing; on her pouting lips there were always vulgarities.

I remember once, I must have been seven going on

eight, when my godfather unintentionally shut the door of the blue Rural Willys on her arm. I heard her curse:

"You cuckold! Pay attention! You almost broke my arm, you cuckold," she repeated.

Could the insult have been a confession? That is what I asked myself when I recounted the incident to Arnaldo, who also complained about her. I never try to remember my godmother, but I must admit the memory comes back to me, unbidden, with a bitter rattle. I don't plan to visit her when I go to Várzea Pacífica, where she lives, now an old lady.

Still May 22
Arnaldo lives on a little ranch very close to the one I bought; I can't remember if I already mentioned this. It's been years since I last saw him, but now we frequently communicate on WhatsApp. I still think of him as my childhood friend, a better companion than Miguel, Clarice's brother, because he used to go everywhere with me, and I was always ready to tag along when he did his farm chores or when he went hunting for *tiús* and *preás*.

I'm certain that time has not changed our friendship. I have little or nothing in common with Miguel nowadays. And I used to consider him a brother! The thing is that children who grow up roaming free on backlands farms, running around barefoot and in shorts, covered with the same mud, made of the same joys and the same misfortunes, have no riches to show off and don't measure each other's material inequalities.

Little by little Miguel began to notice my inferiority: the poverty of my house and my pair of worn-out shoes, even though Mama took such great pains to make sure my sister Zuleide and I were properly dressed for the parties at the big house. Our threadbare clothes were always clean, and when they were white, they were very white; this prompted me to take special care when I sat on the edge of the paths around the big house, next to Clarice, during our childhood games, playing "wireless telephone," whispering messages from ear to ear. Miguel wouldn't have had such worries, because he had a lot of clothes and more than one pair of shoes.

But I wouldn't exchange my life for his. I was tough, he was weak and spoiled. I went out with the cowboys, he stayed on the porch, swinging in the hammock, and as they say, he wouldn't have been able to hammer a nail in a bar of soap. I worked with Arnaldo, going down to the marsh, to the well, to pull weeds or harvest melons. He came with us only very seldom, because Godmother wouldn't let him.

2. Brasília-Fortaleza Flight

June 1

THE PLANE HAS just taken off. It's the Brasília-Fortaleza flight. Now that Patrícia has left me, I'm leaving Taguatinga. I say that she's the one who left me, although I'm the one leaving, since it was her initiative, there's no doubt about that.

She was right and she was brave. I am neither. But I keep ruminating about whether fear sometimes is right. The goodbye was harsh and cold.

"Be happy," she said, as if saying, "Go fuck yourself."

"You too," I answered.

The separation was amicable and there's still a lot to be worked out. She kept most of our possessions, including the house, but she's not asking for money. We've agreed to formalize the divorce but we haven't filed the papers. I suggested waiting awhile, to test how we feel about the separation.

There's no going back; she was firm.

From Fortaleza I'll take a bus through Mossoró and Várzea Pacifica to the little ranch I bought, which I've already named Black Creek, a name that had disappeared from those lands, despite designating the almost dry creek that goes through there and the enormous ranch belonging to my godfather, which was expropriated thirty years ago. In the olden days, it included the small parcel I bought. I could have kept on working as a lawyer representing difficult causes, but after reviewing my finances, I can afford to retire. I just don't have any more savings, which were used to buy the land. Black Creek. For the planting, I'll take out a loan.

I'm going to live there alone. My three sons live far away; I won't speak of them. They are grown men. What's this story about "like father, like son?" One does odd jobs for a living, but thinks he's a filmmaker. I must admit, he was always the most creative one, also the most scattered, unable to concentrate on anything. I worried about him and thought he'd never make anything of himself in life. That's Paulo. The other one, Pedro, is more successful. He's an engineer, the firstborn who gave us—Patrícia, Mama, and I—a lot of work. Especially in his first year of life, he cried a lot, which woke us up at night, and he was always wanting milk, from the breast or the bottle. He grew up to be very competitive, on the street and in school. The two live in São Paulo. We thought, Patrícia and I, that we'd stop with those two. But she forgot to take the pill, and perhaps it was on purpose because she read somewhere that it would have bad side effects, that it could cause cancer. So Teodoro was born. He was always a rebel, troubled. Today he's an assistant manager in a hotel in Fortaleza.

They are different from each other, but they are united in contradicting me. We have contrary opinions basically because I am old and they are young. Or maybe because I had to make my way up from the lowest rung of the ladder, whereas I struggled to give them a start from the highest level and therefore they never knew the difficulties of every beginning. They don't understand how difficult it was to raise them and get them to where they are today. They don't want to see me very often and they never help. Every time we meet, we disagree about something.

But I did let Teodoro know about my trip, and he insisted that I stay in the hotel where he works. He was always special, sensitive, and his nerves showed. He grew up strong and muscular, I think to compensate for the stigma against gay men, especially in the Northeast. We never spoke about the subject. One fine day he introduced me and Patrícia to a friend he was planning to move in with. Just because I was not enthusiastic, he concluded I didn't like the guy.

He was right. I didn't like him for reasons that are hard to explain: a laugh that I didn't trust, a habit of blinking his eyes, and the fact that he didn't talk to me.

"You say you stand up for minorities and are against discrimination but look at what happens at home!" Teodoro flung in my face.

As much as I tried to explain that I had nothing against his choice, I wasn't able to convince him. The idea that I was against their union grew stronger with every untruth that I told to satisfy him, until they separated and he went from one affair to another.

Teodoro was right to move to São Paulo, a big city, where everything is possible, and prejudice dissolves. But now, because of work, he went to live in Fortaleza. I understand that his life isn't easy. He's faced with hellish prejudice. The risk of violence is real; you just have to read the statistics.

Besides being retired, I'll live from planting corn, beans, and even cotton—an absurd idea, I know; nobody needs to tell me. But there is an emotional reason: it reminds me of my childhood. I'll say more about this, without telling everything. In fact, rather than the previous sentence, I wrote some lines I then decided to cross out. If I find the right way to say it, it may be that I'll rewrite them in a new draft.

Now, just practical notes: the area to be planted, which is relatively small, does not justify a big investment for sowing cotton. I won't buy a tractor, at least not in the beginning. I don't even have the money for that. But neither will I go back to the days of animal traction, much less the spade. I've studied this. I saw that the old seed planter can do the job, create uniform rows and reduce the cost of planting.

Gazing at the altiplano from the airplane window—is it the Chapada da Mantiqueira?—I allow another being who lives inside me to appear, another me against whom I've always fought. A sad creature, whose sadness is tender and content, who is relaxed in his own nature. Or maybe it's someone who wants to find the future in the past, I have to admit. We don't have control over what we remember. And what we remember can insist on never going away; it even wakes us up at dawn. It could be on either side of what happened.

Sometimes it's hard to draw the line between memory and imagination. Sometimes reality imposes itself on both. Sometimes the ranch that belonged to my godfather brings up bad memories. The ranch was about three miles from Várzea Pacífica, or Peaceful Marsh, which, when I was a child, was neither a marsh nor peaceful. There the vegetation dried up in the summer—I imagine this still happens—and then for whatever reason, all hell would break loose. There were murders all the time. Terrible murders! Daddy was assassinated with thrusts of a fishing knife. I still see the blood coming out of his belly, spurting, spreading on the ground.

The real memories, when I have them, are vague, of shouts, of doors slamming, of myself running through an endless field. I followed winding and rutted paths, hearing the loud cries of women, of my mother and grandmother, I think. We finally arrived at the place with the hilly ground, marked with crosses, where, next to a bottomless hole, there was a coffin, which I don't know whether I saw or imagined, made of smooth wood and painted black. The mound of dirt next to it also seemed to me like an endless mountain, a mountain I couldn't climb. Tears still fall from my eyes from what I didn't see, I apologize once again to whomever has the patience to keep reading me.

How can I remember this clearly? I was only two years old. I know about the violence of my father's murder because of the stories I heard years later. More than twenty stab wounds from a fish knife, blood running along the sidewalk. Blood, a lot of blood, a red that stains all my memories.

I always thought of that crime when I watched the slaughter of the calves in the corral, seeing the blows of the machete, the strips of flesh and the blood running in streams along the carpet of manure, black and foamy.

The murderer, when he was arrested, never confessed to the crime. A disgusting little guy, a son of a bitch. There's no doubt about it: he had a grudge against Daddy for a trifle—Daddy refused to pay for a leather vest that was poorly made—and he also confessed to the murder of four other victims. He was a bad-tempered guy, irritable, who beat his wife with his fists. His daughter went mad from so many whippings. That's what Arnaldo told me years later, that childhood friend with whom I exchange messages on WhatsApp.

I read once that it's only in the living that the dead exist, just as it will be only in the living that these notes can survive after my death. Daddy is a dead man who lives in me. Why do I want to avenge his death after so long? The truth is I want to. It is becoming more and more of a necessity, the need of an old man, an ever more urgent need, as if I'm missing what I need to do to feel complete.

Merely the thought that I could meet the assassin makes the blood rush to my head. As the days pass, I see that I have little time in which to complete my mission. Of course it wasn't just because of Clarice that I bought the ranch. It was so that I could return to be near the degenerate, the son of a bitch. He left prison several years ago. I never looked for him, but today I know that if I meet him, I'll kill him. I have to kill him. I don't care if I spend the rest of my life in jail. Who would miss me? Not my three kids. Maybe my sister Zuleide. I speak with her so seldom! In fact I haven't seen her in two years. To Patrícia, whether or not I'm in jail makes little difference. She must be happy to be rid of me. And if I die, it will be a glorious death for the best of reasons, believe me or not. I'm carrying a gun in my luggage.

Still on the Plane

We are flying over a storm. The turbulence frightens the young woman next to me. Nervous, she prays in silence.

"Nothing's going to happen," I told her, with a trace of a smile.

Perhaps she doesn't understand how I am able to stay calm and keep writing. I noticed her in the boarding line because she reminds me of a cousin of Clarice's, Luzia, a whole chapter of my sentimental education that I should comment on. I think my words calmed the girl, since she went back to reading on her tablet. I can't see what she is reading. Maybe it's a novel.

"Do you live in Fortaleza?" I asked.

"Yes," was all she answered and she went back to her reading, serious and focused.

I shouldn't say that her mouth is like a frog's because it is pretty and seductive, like Luzia's, Clarice's cousin, who visited Black Creek once in a while. Her lips color her pale face red, a face that fear has turned whiter. Her light well-styled hair is as short as a man's, if you can say that short hair is a man's thing these days. She raised her eyes from her tablet and looked at the back of the seat in front of her. Is she thinking, "What does this old guy want with me?" There are definitely no advantages to old age, and experience, which they say accumulates with time, is of no use to me right now. Old age destroys our body, our muscles, and thank goodness it has not robbed me of my sight, so I can appreciate this young woman's beauty. If she turns to look at me, then she's at least interested in continuing our conversation. I'll wait.

The airplane noise has diminished. It must have reached cruising altitude and I have the impression the plane is flying faster.

Luzia, whom the girl next to me reminds me of, was the only daughter of Uncle Hélio and Aunt Elza. I called them uncle and aunt because Uncle was the brother of my godfather, Clarice's father. They lived in Fortaleza. Once a year, in December, the three of them arrived at the ranch next to Black Creek in a black jeep. Uncle—a coarse man, with a large face and a big nose, who could have been a radio announcer if his deep voice hadn't been so nasal—paraded his shiny red, bald head around the porch of my godfather's big house with a debauched expression and irony in his eyes. I could never hope for affection from him, unless affection can be expressed through orders or guffaws of laughter. Furious orders. Severe guffaws, not trustworthy. I did admire, however, the way he held his cigar, puffing smoke. Aunt Elza was jovial and funny, I understood her charm. She liked to wear bracelets and necklaces and she would strike poses with her rotund, flaccid body, the physique of someone who does not exercise.

One year in particular, I can't remember which, Luzia, who was then about fifteen, seemed more grown up, already a woman, if the size of a bust and a behind can be considered the measure of a woman. Twelve months had made a difference. She had a moon-shaped smiling face, the same rosy cheeks as her mother, and inquisitive eyes. Her starched petticoats puffed out her skirts, which when there was a breeze, lifted up, showing her thighs. She spoke quickly and copiously, with electric gestures. The young woman next to me here has her features, and perhaps that's why I am remembering Luzia. I looked at her. Unlike Luzia, her gestures are measured and her bust and behind, covered by a dress that goes up to her neck and down to her knees, are probably not that big. She smiled at me for the first time, but quickly went back to her tablet, as focused as before.

Everything started on that vacation when Luzia was probably fifteen years old and to me she became the very image of sin. Everything, I mean to say, began with the incident in the cotton storage shed and its conse-quences. My godfather demanded that his children work the cotton harvest, along with the hired hands on the plantation. He said it was so they would learn the value of work. Just studying did not fill anyone's belly. It was important to work and start from the bottom, growing calluses on our hands. I already weeded with the spade and I knew what he was talking about.

But picking cotton was getting off lightly, because when we left the fields Clarice would keep me company. She was skinny, her thin mouth with its sensitive lips traced a line across her face. We would show each other how much cotton we had picked. That time, we stayed late, the cotton fields were turning gray in the dusk, the northeast wind blew cold, and coming back from the harvest Clarice fell on the cotton balls in the storage shed, exhausted at the end of a long day of work. Seeing her so beautiful in front of me, I lay on top of her. Nothing happened in comparison to what I would consider "something" today. She started to laugh, she laughed harder, a nervous, hysterical laughter.

Luzia opened the door:

"What's going on?"

Then she said to me:

"Poor little thing. She's upset. You shouldn't do that."

A strand of Clarice's hair had stayed on my shirt and I kept it like a relic in a little match box.

That same week, when I opened a door to the big house looking for my friend Miguel, Clarice's brother, on a night that the moon rose indiscreetly over the Crooked Arm Mountain Range caressing the landscape with a tenuous light, I ran into Luzia, who was dressed in a white satin slip and a lace bodice. The silence of the night was interrupted by sighs. Sighs that I can hear to this day.

Luzia pulled me toward her and guided my lips to her breasts, which bounced happily out of her bodice. She showed me her erect nipples and told me to suck them like the nipple of a baby's bottle. I did so with pleasure, the sounds of my lapping reaching the ears of the silence. Then she placed my hand between her legs and guided my fragile middle finger into her vagina.

She moaned. She moaned louder. She started to shout, which made me afraid. She pulled me with her strong arms behind the armoire.

Do to me what you did to Clarice, she ordered like a drill sergeant.

Her light skin and green eyes hypnotized me—she could be this young woman next to me, if this one were not timid and could act like a sergeant. I could not repeat what I had done with Clarice, not just because it had been spontaneous and unplanned; also because I could not adjust my body to Luzia's who was much taller than I was.

"So do it with your finger!" she demanded.

She moaned again, louder. Then she slid her body slowly down the wall, pulling me on top of her. She ended up sitting on the floor, and I had fallen down next to her.

An Hour to go before Landing in Fortaleza
There was one more phase of my sentimental education,
one that was not interrupted even by a brief vocation as
a seminarian, which resulted from my sense of guilt. I
said the mass with Clarice and other girls in the pews.
One of them had come because of the floods. The Orós
Dam had burst and flooded her city, Aracati. Her relatives, who were acquaintances of my godfather, stayed
in the big house, and when I saw her, my heart burst
like the breached dam.

Cars rarely arrived at the ranch. The only road, which
was narrow and winding, crossed a river which ran into
the Apodi River and which in the winter carried mud
and branches, imperiling anyone who came near. The
few times that jeeps or trucks arrived, we heard the buzz
of their engines from a distance, at least fifteen or twenty
minutes before they appeared over the top of the hill in
front of the big house. That time, the river would not
allow them passage, and at the top of the hill the family
arriving from Aracati carried their bags on their heads,
the girl in the lead.

I fell in love with that white girl in the white dress.
I sat next to her while she rocked in the swing on the
porch of the big house, supported by columns of *aroe-
ira* pepper trees. Her sweet voice filled the nights with
a melancholy joy. My quandary when I said mass, raising the tea biscuit that served as a host, was whether I
should become a priest or marry her. Clarice laughed at
me. I asked her to be quiet, placing my index finger on
her mouth, and while I raised the host and pointed to

the floor, I demanded that not just she, but all of them, including the girl in the white dress, kneel. Clarice obeyed with a sly look. I confess that I don't know if the girl in the white dress always wore a white dress, but I can't remember her wearing other dresses, just that one, perhaps made of toile or muslin, covered with white embroidery.

Every day at six in the afternoon, we listened to Gounod's Ave Maria in the big house, on the windmill-powered radio. At nine o'clock, before the motor that powered the lights was turned off, we gathered again in the big house and knelt to pray the rosary in front of the wooden oratory, which was built into a corner of the room. The women sang, and my father joined them with a voice that was out of tune. My godmother muttered Paternosters and Ave Marias, swallowing periods and commas and abbreviating words. Father Bosco appeared, along with Padim Ciço and the new phenomenon, Brother Damião, elevating us all to heaven, a placid and undefined sky that contrasted with the hell that was always full of terrible details.

Sometimes strangers came from other ranches or visitors passed through, people who no sooner than they appeared, disappeared for a long time or forever. We would go back to our house, Mama, Zuleide and I, to our red brick house, lit by a kerosene lamp, which cast its tremulous glow over the mud walls. I slept in the living room, moving out of the way of the leaks in the roof when it rained. We had three chairs and a few boxes that also served as chairs when visitors came, whom we received on the porch of beaten clay.

At least once a month we woke up earlier than usual to go to the church at Várzea Pacífica. One day the priest, knowing of my vocation, asked if I wanted to become an altar boy. I accepted and nurtured one of the first great preoccupations of my life: knowing when I had to ring the bell.

The months passed while I remained suspended in my secret hope and Clarice avoided me, smiling obliquely. Until one day, two years after our embrace on the cotton, I thought we would get lost together, we would rise up to heaven, two angels in an eternal embrace. The world would end, Lúcia's secret prediction would come true. Mama cried as she read with difficulty a brochure she had come by on one of our outings to Várzea Pacífica. "I don't know what God's plans are, because I pray every day," she said, with hopes of saving the world.

My heart was as heavy as hers, my throat was constricted. Because of a brochure? I could have torn it up, but I was afraid of revenge. Mama sobbed and wailed. And there was more: before the world ended, we would grow tails on December 31. I believed it and I prayed on my knees that Clarice and I would go to heaven. Or maybe—and then I started to think more clearly—we would go to hell. God and the Pope, His representative on earth, could not be wrong. Everything, animals, men, plants, and even the dams, the rivers, and the stones, would disappear. Clarice and I would go to hell embracing each other.

Later I looked around. Not only had the world not ended, but it was indestructible, made of walls of red brick. Clarice had come to our poor house and we were playing with oxtail bones.

As for Luzia, whom the girl next to me reminded me of, she came back every year. We went swimming in the reservoir spillway, all of us together, and there, on occasion, under the strong, thick, cold jet of water that pushed us together, our thighs grazed each other by accident. I jumped and jumped and hugged her, which excited me, but aside from those few occasions, nothing more happened between us, maybe it was because she had a boyfriend or maybe it was because we didn't have the opportunity.

As far as I can remember, a single better opportunity arose. It must have been the Feast of St. John, because I vaguely remember a square dance when I was dancing with her, after taking slugs straight from a bottle of cheap rum. She was still taller than I was, but inside, bursting into one of the bedrooms, I was able to lift her up and carry her on my shoulders. We fell, separately on the bed. Then she shouted loudly and laughed:

"Help, Clarice, look what's going on!"

I shot out of the room and didn't see her again that night.

3. Fortaleza Beach

June 1

THE GIRL TRAVELING next to me gave me her email.
Her name is Mirna, she is a professor in the Faculty of
Letters at the Federal University of Ceará. I'm glad I
discovered this only after I said goodbye. I'm intimidated
by professors. So she was a literature professor, then? She
would be correcting me and I'm too old to learn.

I said that Mirna looks like Luzia, but maybe that's
not fair to the professor. Let me put it this way: if Luzia
had a sensitive soul, she would be like Mirna. Mirna is
a less full-bodied Luzia, more fragile. She's also different
from Patrícia. Maybe my taste is changing. Damn, I was
attracted to her. Is that crazy?

I should have invited Mirna to dinner then and there.
I didn't dare, and how I regret it! I shouldn't hold back
because of Clarice or Patrícia. Patrícia is the past. Clarice
is the uncertain future. What's real is the bird in your
hand, not two in the air. A conversation in a bar would

be worth it. *Carpe diem.* Take advantage of the good moments.

I just sent an e-mail to Professor Mirna saying I'll be in Fortaleza for two nights and that the day after tomorrow, the third, I'm traveling to Várzea Pacífica. Would she accept my invitation to dinner tomorrow? I don't have much to do here in Fortaleza, except to have dinner with my son Teodoro and to work out the details with the solar energy company installing the panels at the house in Black Creek.

My meeting with Teodoro will be today. He is the assistant manager at this hotel. When I said I would be passing through Fortaleza and invited him to dinner, he insisted that I stay here. I'm not sorry. The hotel has an ocean view, which tonight is not green as our romantic novelist José de Alencar would have liked it. It is a dark sea with points of light in the distance, a passing ship, a landscape that reminds me of a night with Patrícia on top of the dunes at Praia do Futuro.

Teodoro protested when I revealed the purpose of my trip. It's not that he is against my separation from his mother, or because he knows of my plans for revenge or my reunion with Clarice. What he can't accept is that I'm thinking of living on a little ranch in the middle of nowhere.

"You're nuts, whacko," he said, tracing little circles next to his ear. "You won't last a month there."

"It's not in the middle of nowhere. It's close to Várzea Pacífica," I answered without conviction.

The truth is that I don't know what I'll find in Várzea

Pacífica. It's been years since I was there last. It was in 1964 that my godfather moved to his house in Várzea Pacífica with his family. We moved there, too, Mama, my sister Zuleide and I. And Várzea Pacífica changed my life. Up till then I hadn't been to school, even though I was already big. I resisted as long as I could. I suggested that Mama teach me everything I needed to know, but she alleged that one of the reasons for the move was so I could go to school. I was afraid of being locked up for a whole morning in front of a strange woman, having to learn incomprehensible things. Zuleide, a year ahead of me, did not protest.

That Zuleide didn't protest and even liked it was her problem. To me, school was like punishment, the students crowded into a small room, with filthy walls and no furniture, in front of a woman with narrow eyeglasses and long hair, so short she couldn't have been much taller than me. But the fat woman who smelled of lavender and wore flower patterned dresses praised every syllable that I was able to pronounce. I made an effort to respond to her attention, and so I made rapid progress. I started to like books, which my godfather did not approve of. He preferred that I be like his son, my friend Miguel, a practical boy who knew how to count. In school, justice was administered not with pinches, slaps, and boxed ears, like at home, but with a whack from a paddle made of soft wood, a long handle and a rounded tip.

I deserved it and did not protest, but I envied Miguel and Clarice, who went to a private school that wasn't rundown like mine and where they didn't have to take their own stool from home like I did. Their school was in the living room of Dona Antonia's home, the teacher, a single room for all the grade-school students. The house faced a square, where, along with the patio of the church, the social life of Várzea Pacífica took place. That is where the rumors circulated, politics was discussed, more local than national, and at night, on the loudspeaker we heard the music made by one somebody for another somebody.

I confess as I tell this story, I don't have just bad memories of Várzea Pacífica, as perhaps I might have implied. When I stopped by my godfather's house after school, while he had his daily drink of Colonial cachaça, and Miguel had to take his daily bath, I would lie on the parapet of the porch to watch the high school girls go by.

"What a pretty boy," they would say.

"Cute," they repeated.

With my head turned to the road, thinking of Clarice, the girl in the white dress, and mostly Luzia, I waited for the northeast wind to lift their skirts.

Still June 1

Before continuing these notes, I will record one important thing: my meeting with my son Teodoro. This time he was not aggressive with me, perhaps because he had come with his boyfriend, whom he wanted to introduce to me, and was relieved at my reaction. He was perhaps expecting me to evince the macho mentality of someone from Várzea Pacífica or Black Creek. The nice young man also worked in tourism. It's clear they get along well.

They asked if I was still in contact with people
from Várzea Pacífica or the ranches near Black Creek.
Without hesitation, I talked about Arnaldo, Clarice, and
her brother Miguel, who had been my best friend as a
child, almost a brother.

I didn't go into detail. I didn't tell them about my
quarrels with Miguel, or his betrayals. He promised me
things that he didn't deliver. He had what I did not have.
He did not lend me his toys. Pampered, he couldn't
leave the house, when I was always in the street. He
cried over nothing. When he had a cold, he'd go to bed
and godmother would put rubbing alcohol compresses
on his throat.

Once we fought to the point where we hurt each
other. I cut my calf on a stone, which has left a scar to
this day. He told on me and I was severely punished by
my godfather. My godmother, whom I did not consider
my godmother, did not let Miguel go out to get muddy
on the street, build mud bridges and buildings, or sail
paper boats on the river. So I would go to his house and
we'd play in the pointless living room, where visitors
were received and which remained closed with empty
wicker chairs, an icon of Our Lady of Fátima on the
wall with three little shepherds kneeling in front of her,
and photographs of my godparents, Miguel and Clarice
on a table. At my godfather's suggestion, sometimes I
went home with a bag full of black beans that I retrieved
from the storeroom at the far end of the back yard. It's
for your mother's store, he would say.

Yes, I forgot to mention, Mama opened a grocery store in the front room of our new house, which I later found had been arranged by my godfather. It was two streets behind the market, in a narrow building on a corner with a single door and a simple red sign. She spent hours there waiting on customers, arranging merchandise on counters, doing accounts and writing receipts. When we weren't in school, Zuleide and I helped her. On the ground floor in the back were the bedroom, bathroom and kitchen, where we ate around a small square table. What one day was the living room was now the front of the store. Mama slept in the only room on the top floor.

Two streets away from our house was the cobbled main street of the city, which stretched from the city hall to the church. In the dusty side alleys were bars with billiard tables. There, at any hour of day or night, I encountered ragged, prematurely aged people, some of them passed out on the street. I had to jump over puddles of piss on the sidewalks. At the counters, professional drinkers pointed at their glasses to indicate the measure of cachaça they wanted, while they engaged in swearing and fights in which bottles were broken or fish knives were pulled out.

Along the stony streets, carts pulled by donkeys and oxen passed by on their way to market, along with barefoot men carrying sacks on their shoulders. I heard shouts, whistles, the crack of the perverse whips above exhausted animals, and fragments of sentences that I reconstructed, filling in gaps and imagining arguments, intrigues, and love stories. In the market twelve-inch long fish knives were for sale like the one that killed Daddy.

I exchanged a horse for a bicycle, which was a present from my godfather. I felt like a circus performer. I took care of the bike: I lowered the kickstand so the back wheel would be raised and with the pedals I made it spin until the spokes almost disappeared. Then I put oil in the cylinder. I also rubbed oil on the mudguards so they shone. I liked ringing the bell, which sounded like bird song. It was the first object that gave me a sense of ownership. I felt like the owner of something magical and expensive. I didn't care when I fell off the bike and scraped myself up.

Another novelty were the outings to Tibau Beach, ten miles away on the unpaved road that ran through Mossoró, a road full of dust in the summer and potholes in the winter. The imposing hills of red clay led down to the beach, forming chambers, corridors and canyons. Miguel, who by then I considered a brother, and I jumped from the top of the labyrinths where we would hide. We played Western cowboys and robbers shooting imaginary guns. And what a pleasure it was to fall dead on the fine red sand!

We'd also fight, rolling around in the sand. Then we'd go to the beach. We could explore the shallow sea for long distances without the water reaching our necks. I think it was one of those times when Miguel confessed: the boys at school had stuck their dicks in his ass.

Should I believe him? The confession made me wary of his affection.

We would all go to the beach together, my godfather, his wife, who, as I said, was a godmother I did not consider as such, Mama, my sister Zuleide, Miguel and Clarice. Right away on one of the first vacations, Luzia joined us, the one who looked like the girl who traveled next to me, daughter of a brother of my godfather who I called Uncle, a big man with a large face, who intimidated me, and of a woman I thought was funny and whom I called Auntie. Luzia spent the vacations with us without her parents, who had stayed in Fortaleza. Her boyfriend had also come and was staying at the house of some friends. I hadn't forgotten what had happened between us and now I imagined myself capable of doing to Luzia what previously I hadn't been able to manage. I thought of sneaking into her room when we returned from the beach as she was taking off her swimsuit, but there were always people nearby and I didn't have the courage. It also seemed that she had lost interest in me.

I noticed how my godfather looked at Mama, her dark skin molded by the red bathing suit that I thought was indecent and today would consider modest. I felt jealous at such times, and I remembered a scene that I kept reliving in an impressionistic way, since I was not sure that it had happened, just as I don't know to this day. I was so little that I slept in the hammock in the same room as Mama. In the memory that disturbs me most, my godfather, in the bedroom of our brick house would say:

"Maria, we shouldn't do this in front of the boy."

I then noticed that Mama was changing her clothes. She was naked, with her panties pressed between her thighs.

. When we went to the beach, that recurrent scene made me believe there might exist something between my mother and my godfather. But, if that were true, how would it explain that my godmother, whom, I repeat, I never accepted as such, would allow Mama in her house, and what was more, that they seemed to be good friends? Of the two, Mama was perhaps not the most cultivated or intelligent; she knew little more than to read and write. And she was not rich, unlike Godmother. But she was the most refined and beautiful, a beauty that contrasted with my godmother's sour whiteness, and those qualities, which certainly did not go unnoticed by my godfather, were an additional source of worry to me.

I heard indiscreet conversations.

"This is no place to raise children," my godfather shouted.

Despite hearing snatches of stories, or stories told in whispers, one of them I was able to reconstruct clearly: Luzia, now eighteen, had been caught in flagrante doing something forbidden during a party at Urbiratan's house. I knew Ubiratan, he was effeminate, three years my senior. What could have happened?

"Go into the men's room," Luzia said to me, pointing to a public washroom near the beach. "See if they have written anything about me."

I didn't do what she asked. Instead, hearing the noise

of the shower, I climbed up the pipe that went up the
wall joining the men's and women's washrooms. Luzia,
naked, bent over to shield her large, full body with her
hands. She turned away from me and crouched down.
That was the first time I came, not counting masturba-
tions or wet dreams. I fell off the pipe and had to get a
cast on my arm.

She did not complain. On the contrary, she showed
compassion, which moved me. While my arm was still
in a cast, I discovered the reasons for the whispers in the
house. Luzia had been caught practicing with her boyfriend what girls did to protect their virginity. Today I
can say it: they were engaging in sodomy, but the terms
that I heard with an ear to the door were coarser.

The girl who was sitting next to me reminded me
of Luzia only physically. Certainly she is more reserved
and not just because of the dress with the high neckline. The gestures she made while praying indicated that
she must be religious. I sympathized with her, I should
have tried harder to converse. Married? No. At least she
wasn't wearing a wedding ring. Does a ring mean anything these days?

"Are you staying in Fortaleza?"

She simply nodded.

"I'm going on to Rio Grande do Norte," I explained.

Her eyes shone with a mixture of joy and timidity.

It was only later that she gave me her e-mail, to which I
wrote. She's already answered me. She can't tomorrow.
But she gave me her cell number and her WhatsApp

contact, and told me to call when I come back to Fortaleza, which I plan to do, I just don't know when.

June 2, Dawn

I should note that my godfather took good care of his workers' children. He was loving and considerate with Mama, even more than I liked, and for the macho standards of the Northeast, he was a weak man, somewhat feminine in his reactions. Later I understood his aggressiveness; it made his businesses prosper, businesses which today, in the hands of Miguel, his son and my childhood friend, are failing due to problems with the cotton and *oiticica* palm market and the competition from São Paulo and Mato Grosso.

He knew how to earn money thanks to his entrepreneurial spirit and cleverness. He increased production in the cotton oil factory, buying another factory in the area, making donations to electoral campaigns and forming friendships with officials at Sudene, the Northeast Development Bank, so that he could receive financing, and with politicians, so that he could wrangle favors, such as a plot of municipal land on which to expand his warehouses. He also cheated on his taxes, hiring bookkeepers capable of creative accounting. He was a scoundrel, something I recognize only now.

One of his lesser offenses was to claim personal expenses as business expense. The blue Rural Willys belonged to one of the companies. The driver, Mr. Tomás, was an employee of the same company. Mr.

Tomás would drive me and Miguel to the Mossoró salt flats, thirteen miles away; it was open land, smooth, flat, where we saw mirages of lakes formed by the sunrays over the salty ground and white, shining pyramids of salt rising loftily in the horizon. On that plain we could drive the Rural with complete freedom. Every time I stepped on the clutch, hit the brakes or the accelerator, I would sink into the seat and be unable to see what was in front of me.

When our voices broke, Miguel started to get the hots for my sister Zuleide. I tolerated this and tried to control my jealousy. Now my godparents would let him out of the house to play ball with me on the street. He was better at soccer than I was and he protected me when we got into fights with other boys.

He confided secrets to me. Or were they lies to make up for the story he had told me about what the boys at school did to him? Luzia had paraded her big naked breasts around the room where he slept in a hammock, and on a car trip, full of trepidation, she had come on his finger.

"Don't tell anyone," he said to me.

Even though I doubted the story, I was anxious for the chance to travel next to Luzia, the car jostling us along the unpaved road.

Miguel grew a sparse beard; he dressed in expensive clothes, crisply ironed shirts, and shiny shoes that contrasted with my sandals. He seemed like a foreigner, an American Mormon, like the ones who came to the farm to proselytize their religion. His hands, different from mine, were not callused. His thick hair, parted on the side and carefully combed in back, was different than mine, which was curly and unmanageable. Thin, long-limbed, with a high color and eyes full of courage and daring, he had grown up more than I had. He was more easily sunburned than I, who, as I said, have brown skin. He laughed at his own jokes and stories, sure of himself, with the gestures of a future businessman. Whenever he started to brag, he wouldn't stop. He didn't impress me with his vaunted superiority and I started to be proud of my kinky hair. However, it made me very happy when, despite our differences, they said we had the same eyes.

June 2, morning

Looking out at the ocean, feeling the late afternoon breeze, I remember my old times in this city, Fortaleza. When Clarice and Miguel moved here, she to study and he to help with the factory business, both of them living with the brother of my godfather whom I called Uncle, my godfather wanted me to move in with them. I had just turned sixteen and I could help in the house, take care of the yard and also study in a good school. Clarice was a young woman, short in stature, but slender and elegant, and that's why I once affectionately called her a rhea. She had a soft voice and gentle features and she did not relinquish her smile or her delicate manners when talking with me. Everything about her was graceful, even the witchlike features of Godmother, which were perceptible in her long face and nose.

In the beginning I was disoriented by the large agglomeration of houses, buildings, and the streets full of people and cars—today multiplied many times over.

I had imagined returning to the backlands, and to Mama, for the freedom of walking alone in the dusty or muddy alleys. The house stood out on the street: a white cube, protected by a high wall that revealed two iron porches painted blue and large glass windows on the second floor, where my uncle and aunt's room was located.

I no longer found the big house in Black Creek imposing. The floor in the Fortaleza house didn't have a rough cement floor. The sun didn't invade the house shamelessly, because an orange curtain filtered the light that was reflected in the colored mosaics of the living room or the parquet floors of the bedrooms. Two floors of walls without cracks were connected by a narrow stairway. There were no pigs, goats, or children in the yard. Not even a chicken in the backyard, with its coconut, mango, and two hog plum trees.

Uncle wore suits and ties; unthinkable in the backlands. When he sat on the living room couch to read the papers and drink his daily whiskey, and Auntie joined him, announcing her arrival with the jingle of her necklaces and bracelets and the dry click of her heels on the mosaic floor, it seemed to me like a strange television commercial. The television, which was turned on every night in the living room, was the greatest novelty. Our front gate spied on the house across from ours. Vines climbed the iron grates of its wall, which provided a view of the flowers in the garden. I abandoned the television,

Uncle and his whiskey, Auntie and her necklaces, and went to look at the garden full of flowers. The only thing like it I had ever seen was when they took me to the mountains of Maranguape and Guaramiranga.

Here in Fortaleza, the mood of the sea varied as much as the red earth of the backlands. I often went to the beach with Clarice, Miguel, Luzia, and their friends. The sun was as splendid and inquisitorial as an interrogation lamp in a police station, but Clarice did not want to confess what I thought she felt for me. I began to think that my impression was due to a mere projection of what I felt for her, until Miguel's high-school prom, held at the Lebanese Club, when I insisted we become sweethearts, and she seemed to accept me in giving me her hand. But Uncle forbade our relationship without explanation. Auntie added that one day I would understand. I understood right away: I was poor and she was rich.

The following Saturday I walked in the hot sun to the city center, which is a few kilometers west of this hotel. I crossed the Praça do Ferreira and from there continued with no fixed destination along the side streets to the Praça José de Alencar, looking at the stores and the people gathered at the corners. After snacking on a chicken thigh and a Guaraná, I walked around until the late afternoon, when I returned, exhausted. Maybe it was just a question of time. Clarice and I were young and one day we could marry.

Still June 2
Uncle forbade me to take Clarice to the beach, but he
gave me a consolation prize. He invited me and Miguel
to the Clube dos Boêmios, a large house facing the Praia
do Meireles, frequented by various respectable gentle-
men, including him. The young women there did not
look like the whores in the Várzea Pacífica brothel or
even like those who solicited men on the boardwalk in
Fortaleza. Miguel closeted himself in a room with one
of them. I downed a shot of cachaça for courage and
finally approached a big, handsome woman with a book
on her lap.

"What you like?" she asked me, looking up from her
book.

Márcia, which was her name, read romance novels,
love stories, books I wasn't familiar with. The alcohol
helped me lean over her. I had sex for the first time, to the
delight of Uncle and Miguel, who spied on me through
the cracks in the door, they told me later. I don't know
if Uncle had paid for me. Márcia refused payment. I had
sex thinking of Luzia.

Miguel had a girlfriend now, and he went out with her
on weekends. As for me, with the complicity of Clarice
and Luzia, I started going to the beach to meet them
secretly, without the knowledge of my uncles. They
would go by car, with Luzia driving—when she started
studying computer sciences at a private university in
Fortaleza, she had gotten a car—and in the company
of other friends. I took the bus and got off at the usual

stop. I thought Clarice wanted to divert my attention to her friends; to them she introduced me as an old friend of the family, without explaining my subaltern condition.

I felt an attraction to all of those girls, a desire specific to each, but for none of them was my desire as permanent as that which I felt for Clarice and Luzia. The one I thought I could live with for the rest of my life, I soon forgot. Another girl I wanted to make love to one Sunday—not daring to tell her—but the next Sunday I barely felt any pleasure in holding hands with her. One was tall, another was short. One was thin, another was plump. One was dark, another was blond. One talked loudly, another hardly said a word. I forgot all of them.

One of them, whose name I have forgotten, invited me to her birthday party once. I was feeling snubbed by Clarice and Luzia, who pretended not to see me. The guests, with glasses in their hands, walked around the pool, while a young woman sang seductively at the microphone, in a slightly hoarse voice. I thought that she was looking at me, smiling, and that she was beckoning me with the rhythmic gestures of her hands and discreet swaying. I approached her during an intermission. Three caipirinhas motivated me to tell her I had been moved by her singing, that she and her voice were lovely, and that I wanted very much to see her if she would like and when she could.

"Why not now?" she asked.

We went out for a fish stew at a seaside restaurant. It seemed we had lived to meet one day and tell each other our life stories. I said goodbye to her with many caresses on forbidden body parts and a long kiss on the mouth. It was Patrícia.

June 3
On the eve of Luzia's wedding I was alone in my room, sitting at the desk with the radio playing, when Luzia barged in, wearing a yellow dress with buttons all the way down the front. Without saying a word, she started to dance to the music. I got up, went to her, we moved our faces closer to each other, our bellies touched and then we were dancing skin to skin. All those years we had never dared get close to each other, and now she was there, incredibly, embracing me. I was aroused and I wanted her to feel my excitement on her thighs, happen what may, she could refuse if she wanted, I could not hide my desire. Then, to my surprise, she unbuttoned her dress, the only piece of clothing she was wearing. She pulled my hand to her breasts and then between her legs. I came in my black Nycron pants.

"Look at me," she ordered.

"I'm looking, Luzia."

"I'm going to faint," she said, pressing her body closer to mine.

Then we went to the window. I cupped my hands over Luzia's big breasts from behind. She laughed and pushed my hands away. When I started to unbutton my pants, she pushed me away.

"Forget it. Pretend this never happened."

We heard loud footsteps in the hall. Luzia's fiancé and Clarice entered the room, as Luzia composed herself. I tried to pull myself together but I couldn't. I had quickly buttoned my fly, but I could not hide my flushed face. I was afraid they could hear my heart palpitations. Clarice turned and slammed the door and her rage exploded with the sound of her heels pounding the floor outside the room.

The serious young man, with the trimmed beard, stood stock still in front of me. I was waiting for him to punch me in the face. I could not decipher his cold expression of hate or suffering. I closed my eyes, surrendering completely, ready for anything, on the threshold of my own death. I opened my eyes to the same cold stare. I waited for curses, shouts . . . I heard a long, tense silence. I thought of trying to explain, but what? All that was left was to goad him but my words stuck in my throat, they would not come out. He was composed, hiding his fury, if fury it was, perhaps waiting for my first gesture before he reacted or swelling up inside about to explode. With her arms crossed over her dress, which was now buttoned up from top to bottom, Luzia looked at both of us with a frightened expression.

I felt like punching Luzia's fiancé to shatter his icy stare, but he continued to stand silently in front of me, in his pressed long-sleeved shirt, inappropriate for Fortaleza's climate, his perfectly creased pants, shiny shoes, and well-groomed hair parted in the middle. He reminded me of Miguel.

"This is Antonio," said Luzia, introducing him to me

as if nothing had happened and we were at a cocktail party.

Stony-faced, he declined to shake my hand.

"Never speak to me again," Clarice raged at me later.

"Why? I didn't do anything."

"You faker. You piece of shit! Go to hell, get out of my life," she said in a trembling voice, on the verge of tears.

It was sad to witness Luzia's wedding. I did not receive a formal invitation to the party like the others did, but godmother said I didn't need one, I was invited. I remained a spectator, getting drunk on rum, watching the animated party, with live music, and seeing so many guys asking Clarice to dance. I felt sick.

At home it would have been the time for Clarice and me to reconnect, now that Luzia was no longer there, having moved to Natal with her Rio Grande do Norte husband. But Clarice cut off relations with me. She was right not to speak to me.

4. Black Creek

June 10

"You came here to live closer to me but it's as if you were going farther away. I'll never visit you at Black Creek or in Várzea Pacífica, and you can write down what I'm going to tell you: You won't be able to stand living alone out in the bush," Teodoro declared in Fortaleza when we said our goodbyes.

"Who said I was going to live alone? Not alone, but with two employees arranged by Arnaldo, in addition to the company of three tenants on the property," I answered.

And it's true. When I arrived, they were already waiting for me on the porch of my house. I will have comforts. I've even ordered Internet service, forgive me if I'm repeating myself. I feel like I've spent my life preparing for this moment. I'm returning to the place I set out from, no longer a subaltern, but a landowner, even if in size or wealth my property can't compare to the one

my godfather owned. I know that things have changed
with time or rather I've changed my way of seeing them.

One connection to the past will be the cotton. I talked
with the tenants about the planting—it was viable, even
though it was late. It has to be now, urgently. There has
been rain recently and more is forecast, which should
help the seeds germinate. Then the dry season will come,
but if the cotton is well seeded it will not need as much
water to survive. If the boll weevil doesn't ruin my plans,
we'll be able to harvest the crop in October, at the height
of the dry season (which is how it should be, so as not
to compromise the quality of the fiber). We discussed
the spacing and the density of the planting so that when
fully grown, the leaves of the plants will cover, without
interlacing, the entire surface between the rows, which
I've decided will be double rows. We've determined the
number of plants per row and calculated how many
workers I'll have to hire.

I've done many things through the years, but they
would have been wasted years, spent without purpose,
if I hadn't come back to avenge my father and find true
love, and still hadn't been able to prove that some place or
other on earth wouldn't be the same because I had lived.

I had been at risk of getting stuck. How much time
I spent on mere survival! The daily routine was waking
early, going to work, earning enough to feed the family.
Even later, how much energy I spent obtaining the small
pleasures that time ensures we forget. What stands out
are the better times with Patrícia, an uncertain professional success, having helped one or another person with

their issues . . . But has anything really endured from all of that? From the nights of insomnia, the dedication, the meticulous work, the determination to overcome obstacles, and even the dangers? Seventy years! And the children, who don't appreciate the effort and sacrifices made for them! But this is not the time for lamentation. Here, I want concrete things; I want to harvest cotton.

When I arrived at the ranch, the sun illuminated the green landscape, not the new green of incipient winter, but green nonetheless, now a dark green. Soon I was overcome by weakness, as if I had lost everything I had patiently conquered over the course of many years in order to insert myself into a past to which I could never return. Out in the bush! Could Teodoro be right? It was late afternoon. As I lost myself in such thoughts, shadows settled over the trees. They leached their unity, greying every hue, flooding the world. Then the stars came out; in the darkness of the night, they perforated the sky with doubts and anguish. I know it will take time for everything to become clear and for the results of my new work to reveal themselves.

The land I bought includes the old ranch house, I don't know if I've already mentioned this, a house that I had thought was imposing, but which today seems humble. The terrace, to the right of the entrance, where I picked sweet grass with Clarice, which we sucked on like candy, was not as long as I remembered. The entire house was not as large as when I used to come here. The irregular, dirty whitewashed walls have cracks and holes through which lizards scuttled. The living room, covered with cobwebs, still has its wooden hammock hooks, but the chests are gone. The dining room is missing its long, worn table of solid wood. The four bedrooms and the hallway where Dona Leopolda, Clarice's grandmother, used to keep her sewing machine, seems to have shrunk.

The dark kitchen, with its red, irregular plaster walls, still has the wood stove. The bare sucupira beams need replacing. Next to the house are the remains of the lean-to where the saddles and bridles of the horses were kept. I was happy to see that the tamarind tree was still in the back yard. The mill house, whose small mill was disused even when I was a child, still houses the wooden axel and spokes that in past times were moved by oxen. When I was a child, it was there that they used to pour syrup into molds to make sugar cane candy.

The new house is about two hundred yards from the old big house, and has an enormous mango tree in front. Modern and poorly constructed, I did not immediately notice its defects, which are now obvious. There is no back door. The only side with a porch is too hot in the afternoons. There are no half walls or openings for ventilation; they told me it was to prevent bats from flying in at night from the trees in front. The door of one of the rooms does not close properly. I want to ignore these defects, and see it as my own house, with modern comforts: electricity, a parabolic antenna, telephone, and soon Internet, in addition to the solar panels. That's enough for me.

The few pieces of furniture were delivered by a moving company owned by an acquaintance of mine from

Taguatinga, who is also from the Northeast. I still have to unpack them. Even my collection of matchboxes, metal boxes, and the stamp collection that I kept over the years have arrived. They must all be in the chest of drawers that I asked the movers to place in my bedroom. In one of the drawers is a strand of Clarice's hair in a matchbox.

In front of the big house the stones on the hill where I scraped my knees in front of Clarice no longer exist. They've built a narrow road there, which is already full of potholes. To the west, where as far as the eye could see there wasn't a single house, and the flatness was inter-rupted only by a wall of mountains, now you can see a conglomeration of houses, and near one of them, a reservoir surrounded by a large green area. Mr. Rodolfo, Arnaldo's father, had a house on Uncle's property, where his beautiful wife Victoria would plant herself in the window. It too has disappeared. The well where Gray used to go to fetch water, which is close by, is still there, but today a pump delivers water through pipes to the house.

I tried to get back in touch with my childhood friends. Almost nobody lives here any more. Mr. Rodolfo partic-ipated in the Landless Workers Movement and led the expropriation of the farm. I don't even know if he's still alive; I should have asked his son, Arnaldo. And Dona Vitória, might she preserve traces of her former beauty? My godmother, who I said wasn't like a godmother to me, lives in Várzea Pacífica and is ninety years old. I don't want to visit her, I repeat. Of my old friends, the only one who lives in the area is Arnaldo, my childhood hero, whom I consider to be a good man, honest and less ignorant than I would have imagined someone who has only gone to grade school. I don't mention Clarice, because I don't need to talk about the obvious.

My only enemy also lives near here, a person I barely know, but whom I have heard about ever since I can remember. My father's murderer. I said that if I found him, I would kill him and I don't give a shit if I go to prison for the rest of my life. It bears repeating that I will confront him; there is no doubt years of jail don't erase a heinous crime.

My childhood friend Miguel, Clarice's brother, who for years divided his time between Fortaleza and São Paulo, now lives in Várzea Pacífica trying to save the factories from ruin, after rescuing them from bankruptcy. When Patrícia and I moved from Fortaleza to the Federal District, I don't know whether I've said so already, I started to limit my contact with him to one call a year at Christmas and an occasional exchange of letters, which were then replaced by infrequent emails. I can count on my fingers the number of times I've met him, usually when I was in Ceará on vacation. The truth is that I've changed with time, whereas he hasn't. Our differences have grown—differences of politics, of opinion—even if he's become less rich and I less poor. Do we even belong to the same species of human being?

Once I wrote to tell him: Now I'm a lawyer and I live in Taguatinga. He wrote back congratulating me and asked after my sister Zuleide.

Of course, Zuleide! Still Zuleide! He hadn't changed; he still had no shame or sensibility. I could have explained that Zuleide lived in Recife, that she was married to a good husband, a doctor, and was the mother of five children. I didn't even answer. Zuleide, the only person—thing—that interests him to this day, a voluptuous black girl, not pretty, but with long legs and thick thighs the way he said he liked them. When we lived in Fortaleza, Miguel had sucked Zuleide's nipples when she spent a few days with us. Her breasts were young and firm during that time of our adolescence, and he was two years older than her.

"I've never seen such beautiful breasts," he whispered, holding them in his two hands.

"You're not the first one to say that," she answered.

I know this because I watched the scene through the slats of the bedroom window that looked out on the back porch where they were locked in an embrace. Without revealing that I had witnessed the scene, I started to threaten him. He should not dare to get near Zuleide or he'd have to deal with me. He replied by telling me that I'd better not go near Luzia; he knew I had the hots for her. I backed off. It was a trade, my sister for Luzia.

June 10, Night
The misunderstanding between Miguel and my godfather increased with time. After years of a fortune that expanded and retracted like an accordion depending on

whether there was a good harvest or a drought, my godfather started to wither, and his white beard and hair
looked like cotton pulp. He let his son take the reins
of the businesses and introduce new technologies along
with stricter management of the employees. Unlike him,
Miguel was not generous to those who needed help.
My godfather would swing in the hammock, accept-
ing defeat, and he abandoned Mama to her fate when
the Várzea Pacífica grocery store started to lose money,
which forced her to move to Mondubim, on the outskirts of Fortaleza, near the house of the people she had
met in Várzea Pacífica and who had shown her the ropes.
She sold the house and the store in Várzea Pacífica and
opened a small shop. At her request, I left Uncle's house
is Fortaleza and went to live with her behind the shop,
helping her with the business.

We didn't talk much. Although I thought I knew the
answer, I asked her one day:

"Why did you want to leave Várzea Pacífica, ma'am?"

I always called her "ma'am."

"It was better that way. I don't depend on anyone
any more."

That was all she revealed and I didn't ask again. It
must have been to do with my godfather, I thought.
Who else could it have been? Hadn't we lived on his
ranch? Hadn't he been the one who had helped her open
the grocery store in Várzea Pacífica?

It was better to be independent, I agreed, although
it was not at all easy to make a living from the damned
shop. The difficulties were huge. The shop opened early

and closed late. We invented stuff to sell, and if someone didn't find what they wanted, we would do whatever it took to satisfy the customers and keep them. We went without sleep to earn a few more cruzeiros, eating little to make the money last. It would still be dark when we woke up. At night I'd hang my hammock near the front door, so that I'd wake up if a customer arrived after hours. If that happened, Jaguar, our skinny, brownish yellow mutt, would bark loudly. When we were able to scrape together some money, I bought an old car, which cost a lot to maintain, and broke down frequently, forcing me to walk and to learn something about mechanics.

I passed the college entrance exams, almost failing Portuguese. I went to Law School at night. That was the beginning of another difficult road. Later, with my diploma in hand, I would have to fight hard to get a job. I did not get one through straight lines, but crooked lines are sometimes drawn by God. I accepted work that had nothing to do with my degree and I almost gave up the Law. However I had passed the Brazilian Bar Exam and I thought I should persevere. That way, controlling my impatience, I was able to put the worst defeats behind me.

One day, I attended the funeral of Uncle, Luzia's father, the brother of my godfather, who owned the next ranch over from Black Creek. Miguel told me that the cause of death had been financial ruin; the death certificate signed by a doctor friend listed heart attack as the *causa mortis*. The life insurance policy did not cover death by suicide.

Clarice came to the funeral without her husband. We hardly spoke but we exchanged sad looks. Before leaving, I gave her a tender hug, and her eyes filled with tears.

June 16

Clarice is now a widow, have I already said that? Her husband died more than five years ago. I met him. He was a nice guy. The encounters were few and always intense. One time we went to Prainha, near Fortaleza, to eat crab. Then we walked on the beach, feeling the waves on our feet. There was a strong breeze, and Clarice gave me a few beautiful shells that she had found. Another time Clarice and he invited me for a weekend to the ranch near Black Creek. That time I noticed him trying to disguise his jealously, saying offhandedly that Clarice always talked about me and admired me.

I sincerely don't know what he did other than take care of the ranch. I didn't ask him or Clarice. It was enough to know that he was part of that small universe of rich people who dominate our world, ignoring the poverty around them. I forgave him for being married to Clarice, she was so different from him. If she hasn't changed, she still considers herself as being on the left, indignant about poverty and inequality; at least that's what I remember. It's not her fault that she was born into a rich family.

Even in front of her husband, she took certain liberties with me, calling me to accompany her to the kitchen, putting her arm around me, laughing at the stupid things I said and reminiscing about our childhood games, which left me flustered.

Maybe when I see her it will be like a cold shower, we might not have anything in common. On the other hand, I must admit, what happened isn't over. One of the reasons for my return, which must be perfectly clear now, is to meet her. More than that, if there are reasons that tie me to the world, Clarice is one of them. She gives me the courage to face the difficulties, which are not few, of my return. I know she also wants to see me again, otherwise why would she have written that e-mail? Otherwise why would she have accepted my friend request on Facebook and then sent me a message again with her cell number? When I arrived almost a week ago, I sent her an e-mail. I still haven't received a reply. I should call.

June 18
I know that I have come in search of a time that is gone. Has it changed for the better or the worse? Maybe both. At Black Creek there is now electricity twenty-four hours a day, paved streets, Internet, and almost everyone has a cellphone. There was none of this in my childhood, just a lot of dust and mud. Nevertheless, as I looked around when I arrived in this town that used to be mine, it was the same old poverty, just more spread out. Where there were fields and dryness there are poor neighborhoods that are immune to the political winds and the different schools of interpreting reality, some devouring others,

and none of them capable of changing the interior of this country in a profound way.

When I started walking down Avenida Central, I didn't see the Várzea Pacífica of today, because everything I saw was with the eyes of the past. I was blind and deaf, because attention precedes the senses. Little by little my attention allowed the times to mix, with elements of the present being assimilated by the past. Children walked past me, laughing and talking. I had the impression that two of them were talking about me. I imagined myself as a child looking at an old guy like myself walking the city streets. Would those children of today view me with the same respect and fear with which I viewed old people when I was a child?

I don't think so. Children today are more adult, independent, and think they know more than old people. Do any of them lie on their front porches to look at the girls on the sidewalk as I did? Do they wait for the wind to pick up their skirts when all they have to do is go to a computer to see a lot more?

It was sad to walk along the main street where carts still circulated, to pass by my godfather's old house, my school, Clarice and Miguel's school, to climb up to the porch of the church to get a general view of the town. I entered the church. The saints are the same, the same altar at the back. I saw myself as an altar boy during mass. I knelt, as I had not done in a long time, but I did not pray. The silence was broken only by the footsteps of a devout woman who seemed to have come from the past and who made the sign of the cross. I had the sensation that it was an acquaintance frozen in time. I left, dizzy, wandering along the side streets until I came across the ruins of our old house and grocery store on a dirty corner. I felt like talking to that wall, my wailing wall, which knew how to listen to my secrets.

Since I had learned that Miguel was in town, I looked for him at the factory. He received me in his office. He was cold and formal, despite pats on the back and forced laughter over almost nothing, or rather, my plans to plant cotton. He already knew about my purchase of Black Creek, my separation from Patrícia. He asked about Zuleide. I limited myself to saying she was still in Recife with her husband and that the five children were doing well. I stayed just long enough to drink an espresso. I felt there wasn't much to talk about. Even so, we agreed to meet again and exchanged cellphone numbers.

"Come visit the house at Black Creek," I suggested.

"Yes, I will. For sure. I'll let you know."

June 19

The Black Creek ranch is, of course, not the way it was when I was a boy. Uncle's land has been parceled out. Not even the big house remains standing. Mr. Rodolfo, Arnaldo's father, is dead, as I had thought. At some point he had become an owner of a piece of the old Black Creek ranch—a small one to be sure—a piece that Arnaldo inherited. Vitória is still alive and remembers me, Arnaldo told me. I might visit her one day.

Luzia does not visit these lands anymore. She never

separated from her husband, contradicting my prediction. One of her sons was arrested for drugs. I don't
know what has become of him. After Luzia got married
I ran into her once by chance in Fortaleza. She had lost
her beauty, despite her flowing hair and the swish of her
red skirt. Her suntanned skin was covered with spots.
She had gained weight. A lot. To be nice, I said "We
have to get together." She looked at me in disgust, as if
I had made an indecent proposal.

"What are you thinking? Get a grip, guy."

June 30

The day before yesterday I went to Várzea Pacífica to
look for Daddy's assassin. In my pocket I carried the gun
I had brought in my baggage and I also wanted to buy a
fishing knife like the one he used to kill him. That's why
I went to the market, which was still in the same place,
near Mama's old grocery store where today there is a bar.
I didn't want to walk around with that big fish knife.
I tossed it into a bag to avoid attracting attention. My
heart pounded as I walked toward the murderer's leather
store, not sure what was going to happen or whether I'd
use the knife or the gun.

It was noon, the sun was at its zenith and the heat was
suffocating. From a distance I saw the store sign, which
was crumpled and poorly made, with black lettering
against shiny metal that looked more like graffiti. The
street had little commercial traffic. Two stores were open,
a grocery store and a pharmacy. The doors and windows

of the rest of the buildings, all residential, were shuttered. I walked with slow steps, trying to gauge the gravity of what I was about to do. I encountered just one woman, carrying a bag like mine, certainly a future witness against me in a criminal trial. My certainty that I was not afraid to spend the rest of my life in prison began to weaken. If I were arrested, would I lose Clarice forever?

However, there was a chance of committing the murder without being arrested, a murder like so many others that happen in Brazil and which are never solved. I would make my decision about what to do and how to do it once I arrived at the leather store. I was certain of just one thing: the son of a bitch would know I why I was there.

I saw him from a distance, at the back of the store which was situated in a narrow building. I noted a crack on the white façade, which had been tinted gray by the rains. A flight of three steps led from the sidewalk to a wide-open door. I approached slowly expecting that he would see me. He solemnly ignored my presence, even when I stopped in front of him. He kept hammering at a piece of leather, with a steady rhythm, like an automaton. His jowls were sunken into his long face and his skin was completely wrinkled. He was scrawny, an ugly man without a smile or any other redeeming feature.

I had come with a clear purpose. I could not fail. I shouldn't weaken.

"Do you know why I'm here?" I finally asked him, after a few minutes of silence during which I watched the regular blows of his hammer on the leather.

"If you wish, and if you pay . . ." he answered drily, certainly not understanding what I was saying, without raising his eyes and smelling of cachaça.

"I'm not here to order a leather vest. I'm Adalberto's son, the man you killed, you shit!"

With my bag in my left hand, I put my right hand over the gun in my pocket, still not sure what I was going to do, if I was really going to shoot him.

He raised his arm with the hammer in his hand. I had the presentiment that he was going to hit me in the forehead. I tried to hold his arm. The hammer flew out of his hand, slid across the floor, fell down the stairs and landed at the feet of a woman passing by on the sidewalk.

"What's going on you old fool?" she shouted.

He was able to free himself from my grasp, pushing me against the wall. As he was running toward the sidewalk he tripped and fell, hitting his head on the corner of one of the doorsteps. He fainted.

The woman, who was still standing on the sidewalk, made a call on her cellphone to the only hospital in Várzea Pacífica. We stood there for about a half hour. People gathered. I was screwed. The number of witnesses was mounting. But what could I do? Finally, the ambulance took my father's murderer away. He still appeared to be unconscious.

The woman confirmed my version of the facts. It had been an accident. The crazy old man had been startled by my presence, he attempted to hit me with his hammer, and he tripped. Nobody would file a complaint with the police, except him, if he regained consciousness. Who would stand up for the wretch? A family member? He was alone, she said.

I still think to myself: would some human rights organization be interested in this case? I conclude that such a thing does not exist in Várzea Pacífica. It's up to me, a man of principles, to defend him, to take the guilty person—that is myself—to court. But nobody is obliged to be their own hangman. My principles bend to circumstances. They have to mold themselves to the fact that they are being applied to an assassin, a cold and calculating assassin, a despicable being who does not deserve my respect, my consideration, and much less my pardon.

July 14

The story spread and reached Arnaldo, the friend who lives on the ranch next to mine. Without rebuking me, he told me that the poor fool's wife had left him a long time ago. He has a crazy daughter who lives in an asylum in Fortaleza. He is poor and illiterate. He had rehabilitated himself. No other crime had been attributed to him since he left prison. He's certainly over ninety years old and it shows, he said. He still works hard, fixing saddles and making leather vests, the only trade he knows, but in this he has become a skilled artisan. Since he was never taught, he developed his own methods to select and soften the leather and to make hard-wearing vests. And now, what was going to happen to the poor man? He was still unconscious in the hospital.

Listening to that story, I felt like a wretch who was destroying the life of another wretch.

Arnaldo then said there was something very serious that I ought to know. What? I asked, frightened. I had to get in touch with Raimundo, a hired killer I'd known as a child. No matter how much I insist, Arnaldo says it's not his place to tell me. I need to hear the story from the source and draw my own conclusions.

I remember Raimundo well. I was feeling proud because they'd let me go on horseback by myself for the first time, to buy fish from Arnaldo's father, Mr. Rodolfo. He was, as I said, the husband of the lovely Vitória and a tenant of the neighboring ranch, Uncle's property, the one with the reservoir where the mute girl would go swimming naked. I wanted to show off my new horsemanship skills, making the horse go from a cantor to a gallop. Mr. Rodolfo fished in the reservoir and was the best horse tamer on the ranch. I had the job of carrying the fish, which I did regularly from then on and which gave me pleasure, not just to show off my horsemanship but also because I liked to see the smile and the body of Mr. Rodolfo's wife, Arnaldo's mother, whose light dresses barely concealed her curves. Vitória was attractive, and she smiled at me. Even when I didn't stop, I would go by her house just to catch a glimpse of her in the window.

That day I raced back to the big house, carrying the fish in a sack tied to my saddle, eager to show off my skill as a horseman. To my surprise, the gate to the property, which was beyond a curve in the road, was closed. The horse, which had been running wildly, reared abruptly and I was thrown forward, where I was able to hang on around his neck. I had never been so close to death. At that moment, Raimundo appeared, also on horseback. He immediately dismounted to help me, calming my horse.

Arnaldo then told me that Raimundo, a cold killer, was a hitman contracted by the landowners. It would be advisable not to cross him. Arnaldo knew everything. Raimundo had several murders to his name, but he would never go to prison, since he was protected by several ranchers.

I remember him very well, he was one of my godfather's best friends, and they say he had also been a good friend of Daddy's. He had a delicate smile that revealed rows of yellowed teeth. I came to respect and fear him. I saw him many times arriving at the porch of the big house, tall, thin, sunburned, with long hands and nose, light hair and eyes like an owl. He had a soft voice, and wore boots and spurs, whose rosettes jingled to the rhythm of his long strides. There was a vague sentiment of affection when he ran his hands through my curly hair as if he wanted to muss it up, always with that delicate smile. He treated me well.

"He's a good guy," Arnaldo said to me.

September 7

It was a week ago. Mounted on his horse, making his spurs jangle, Raimundo leaned against the verandah of the house and said in his soft voice:

"They created a Truth Commission and before I die, I want to take a weight off my conscience. Of all the deaths on my shoulders, I regret only one. It was ordered by your godfather."

He told me: Daddy, on orders from my godfather, set fire to the cotton storehouses. It was a job well done, which earned my godfather good insurance money. Two years later Daddy started to make demands, and some were about me. He wanted money to move his family far away. He wanted me in a private school when I grew up so I could go to university.

It was this bandit who, on orders from my godfather, killed Daddy, he confessed. Raimundo had doubts about whether or not to kill his friend on a contract from another friend. Now he had doubts whether to denounce his old friend, my godfather. If I believe what he says, then my godfather killed Daddy because of blackmail. I have to decide if I believe it. The clusterfuck had reached a new level.

Never in my life could I have associated my godfather with that kind of crime. Dodging taxes, bribing the mayor—that would be normal, expected. I remember hearing him say that money was well spent on buying votes and throwing parties for candidates. He distributed dentures and brought a doctor from Mossoró to give free exams before the elections. His political party was always the one that could win power or was already in power.

But kill a friend? He practically adopted me when I was just two years old, me and Zuleide, my sister, who was four by then. Should I call Recife and discuss the matter with Zuleide? I frankly don't know what to do. I don't have any reason to disbelieve what the gunman told me. Should I talk about it with Clarice? With Miguel?

I wrote above that I have to decide whether I believe it. Well, I don't have to decide. It's decided. I believe it.

September 27
I called Clarice. She was so enthusiastic, welcoming me, inviting me to visit, that I did not have the courage to tell her the main reason for the call. I promised to visit soon, soon, but I couldn't set a date. I should visit her and think about how to introduce the subject.

Last night I couldn't sleep, thinking of the crime committed by my godfather. Today the idea hit me again that my godfather had been having an affair with Mama. I think it's plausible that I am the son of my godfather; that he is my father. I looked in the mirror trying to find his features in mine. They are obvious, despite the difference in skin color. It makes sense that several people saw the resemblance between me and Miguel, evident not just in the eyes, but in the shape of the face and chin. The worst thing is that if this suspicion is confirmed, then I'm Clarice's brother. I conclude that bad things are on a scale and I can't see one that is worse. Of course, it's still mere suspicion. If we don't do DNA tests, we won't know for sure if we're brother and sister.

I don't know what to do. I look in the mirror again.

In fact I look like my godfather. Should I tell Clarice what I suspect? It's decided, I'm going to meet her this week.

The person I thought was my father was killed, perhaps because on the orders of the person I think is my real father, he set fire to the cotton mill and then tried to blackmail his boss with ever greater demands. Or perhaps he threatened to kill him out of jealousy and my godfather anticipated this and had him murdered.

Jealousy, the real reason for the crime! Jealousy! I see it now clearly.

My feelings about my godfather are confused. Either he is a cruel murderer, or a caring father who raised me. It doesn't matter that he almost abandoned me when Mama left Várzea Pacífica and I went to live with her at Mondubim.

October 1
Arnaldo has brought me up to speed on local politics. I don't have a knack for this, I said. I remember the old days when whomever Miguel supported won the election. In this he followed in his father's, my godfather's— who was maybe also my father—footsteps. In Várzea Pacífica the alternation of parties took place in the same family. But now the situation was different. There are groups that he, Miguel, could never control, connected to the Landless Movement and other social movements. Arnaldo says that Miguel's candidate doesn't stand a chance, that Miguel is an unpopular guy; he doesn't want to waste time with humble people.

The opinions on each side are passionate. They all hate each other, is what I conclude, and alliances are forged not through a convergence of ideas, but through shared hatreds. There is a lot of unrest, and it's good that some leave and others enter, but I have the impression that when the wheel turns and the roles are inverted for those above and below, the discontent might fester.

We are at the edge of the abyss, I hear from the pessimists. We are at the bottom of the well, say the optimists. Since I've often heard this in the uproar during crises, I don't latch on to any one savior.

From my time in Fortaleza, I remember that Uncle was also interested in politics and that his opinions changed depending on the editorials in the paper. Sometimes he defended a strong state, capable of ending ignorance, poverty and violence; sometimes he was for minimum state interference, which would not mess with things. He liked to complain that the system was failing.

"What's going on, man? Are you losing money?" Aunt would ask.

For her, since governments were always transitory, even if they thought they could control the world into the future, it wasn't worth beating yourself up for them or even fighting them.

"Life is too short for people to waste time with this nonsense, fighting over politics," she grumbled, avoiding the discussions.

"In politics, the lie told with conviction becomes truth, and the ones who lie the most win the most," she said one day.

And she repeated the idea another way:

"A lie that many defend becomes the truth."

As for Luzia, it didn't matter what the topic of conversation was, she was always on the other side. It was possible to transform hell into heaven, you just needed the will to do it. With Uncle changing his mind whenever a government rose or fell, she took radically contrary positions to those she had assumed in times past and that way became her most fervent opponent.

Time itself, in my opinion, goes by without concern for these variations, things that are born from their opposite, which fold and unfold, which come and go or become entangled.

I hope the laws improve and that rival factions debate in a free and organized manner, so that people learn what is best for Várzea Pacífica. I remember Miguel was called a bourgeois. Now they accuse him of being a strongman, corrupt, conservative, on the right, even a fascist. The last time we discussed politics, he raged against the opposition, which he thought represented ignorance and radicalism. But I agreed when he admitted that at every level politicians were rats, who could smell money, and that few truly cared about the country.

I've already decided, despite Arnaldo's insistence, that I'm not going to get involved in these discussions. I'll focus on making Black Creek a working ranch. But things move slowly. I don't know how the cotton harvest will turn out, which now won't be until October. At least it won't depend on the irrigation system, which I wasn't

THE LAST TWIST OF THE KNIFE

able to find a solution for. I've incurred more expenses than I imagined. On the positive side, the Internet and the solar energy panels are working properly.

October 4

I found out that Raimundo—the hitman who sought me out to tell me that my godfather, who I think is my father, killed the man I previously thought was my father—was shot with a gun. Certainly it was to silence him. If he opened his mouth about my godfather— that is, my father—he could do the same with others, enough reason to shut him up forever.

But the police investigations point in another direction. He was fighting off a mugger. A household worker confessed being party to the crime and was put in jail. For the police, the matter is settled. Not for me.

5. Várzea Pacífica

October 29

I DIDN'T KNOW I would get into such a big fight with Clarice and Miguel. First, I went to visit my godmother, who I never had considered to be my godmother. If anyone knew that my godfather was my father, she would be the one. The shriveled old woman protested against my suspicion, in a barely audible but energetic voice. Her effort was obvious. She flew into a rage, she was shaking, the veins popping out on her face. She almost died. The worst thing is that a few days later she really did die, not because of me, but Clarice and Miguel blamed me.

I suggested they take a DNA test. They were outraged and continued to accuse me of killing their mother. I concluded they didn't want the truth to come out so they wouldn't have to share the heritance.

"Don't you want to know if you are my sister?" I asked Clarice, who turned a deaf ear.

The only recourse was through the law, and I've been

at this for almost a month. I filed a paternity suit along with a claim to the inheritance. I decided to act as my own attorney in court, without hiring outside counsel. I also searched in vain among the things I brought in the move to the house at Black Creek to see if, as I thought, the matchbox in which I kept a strand of Clarice's hair had arrived along with the other items in my collection.

First, I filed a suit with the judge. I alleged that the relationship between my godfather and my mother was strange, he was always protecting her, our family moved to Várzea Pacífica when he moved, he helped with opening the grocery store, sent me to Fortaleza with his children, treated me like a son. I also presented the crime he had committed, according to the testimony of the hitman, adding the obvious:

"All children have the same rights under the law."

Finally I stated the impossibility of a post-mortem exam, since my godfather's ashes had been thrown into Black Creek (even though Clarice had said she kept some of the ashes), and that the situation required that Miguel or Clarice take a DNA test.

Clarice and Miguel responded through their lawyer. What I considered indications of infidelity was proof of generosity. If my godfather had thought me his son, he would have taken responsibility for it while still alive and listed me in the will. They alleged that the suit to make them submit to a DNA test was not based on reasonable motives. The defendants could not be compelled to submit to such an invasive examination. There was no law to force them to do so.

In my response, I cited the relative presumption of paternity, based on a new ruling of the Supreme Court of Justice, which states that in an investigative action, the refusal to submit to a DNA test leads to a *juris tantum* presumption of paternity.

The judge understood that the judgment I cited only would be applicable under two conditions: that the heirs, in an unjustified manner, had refused to submit to the DNA exam, a condition that had been fulfilled, and that there were other proofs, or rather, in the case in question, coherent and sufficient testimony to permit the conclusion regarding biological parentage. The second condition was not a given. The broad array of probative evidence had to be taken into account. It wasn't possible to assign to the refusal itself the robust nature that the plaintiff, that is, I, attempted to give it. He spoke of his moral certitude and a judicial opinion based on reason and analysis of the circumstances, and that certainty and opinion led him to reject the possibility I alleged. If need be, he would gather testimony, but first there would be a mediation meeting.

November 12
In the courthouse—a building with blue walls full of cracks and stains, on the same street as the church, not far from the house of Miguel's old private tutor, Dona Antonia—I put forward my arguments to counter those of the defendants' lawyer, a guy half my age with a shaved head, the face of a weasel, and an unnecessarily

pompous voice. There was a discussion about whose rights should prevail: the right of the plaintiff to his real identity or the right of the defendants to their physical inviolability. I made it clear that the right to inviolability of the body was not absolute. I gave as an example obligatory vaccination for the sake of public health. The right to genetic identity should prevail over the principle of the inviolability of the human body and the plaintiffs' right to physical integrity. Furthermore it was ridiculous to speak of physical inviolability since all that was needed was a strand of Clarice's hair for proof, and that strand of hair I had, I just didn't know where it was. I hadn't found the matchbox where I kept it. To speak of the plaintiffs' physical integrity was a joke; my right to know who my father is should take priority, and five milliliters of blood, a drop of saliva or a strand of hair could resolve the problem without violating the physical integrity of Clarice or Miguel in the slightest. I grew heated and argued in vain. In face of this stalemate the judge set a hearing to collect the testimonial proof that he deemed necessary.

December 13

The only witness I could get was Arnaldo. At first, he resisted.

"Your mother was a saint. Do you want to ruin her reputation?"

After much insistence, he agreed to appear in court. He was the first to be heard. He said that he had known

me and my mother since I was very young, that Mama
was an upright woman, he couldn't say if she had had an
affair with my godfather, but it was true she was always
in the big house and that my godfather treated her dif-
ferently than the others; that my godfather sometimes
went to her house, which he did not do with any other
woman; that if Mama had an extra-marital relationship
it wouldn't have been with anyone except my godfather, who treated me like his own child. In the end he
exaggerated in saying that if you looked closely not only
was it a case of physical resemblance, but I was the very
spitting image of my godfather.

The defendants' lawyer roped in several witnesses,
who attested to the chaste life of my godfather, a man
of impeccable reputation, happily married to my godmother and incapable of lying or committing the slightest infidelity. These people said they had known my godparents their whole lives, for fifty years or more. One of
them offended me deeply by insinuating that I had reason to suspect I was not Daddy's son, since my mother
was not an honest woman, and had never been, that
honesty is something you're born with. She had more
than one lover, none of them my godfather. She had
gotten pregnant before me and lost the child.

A woman with straight, completely white hair said that
my godparents' marriage was exemplary. There had never
been talk of my godfather having affairs. He was not the
kind of man to hide the truth about a child. If I had been
his son, he would have filed my birth certificate. It was a
joke to say that I looked like my godfather. It was enough

to see the color of my skin. I was dark compared with my godfather's white skin. That absurd argument burned me up since it didn't take into account Mama's skin color.

A third witness, a soft-spoken man with a nasal voice, whom I couldn't remember ever having seen either on the ranch or at the house in Várzea Pacífica, said he was a good friend of my godfather's, he had been close to him for forty years; that my godfather and godmother, when I was born, were like two young lovers; that like the previous witness, he had never heard any talk of affairs; that he and my godfather were intimate enough to confide in each other and my godfather had never mentioned having a child out of wedlock.

The fourth witness was a well-preserved woman in her late sixties. She said she always had the impression—and it was a general impression, shared by many—that my godfather was a very faithful man, perhaps like no other on the face of the earth. The only doubts that had been raised—which were slander, pure slander—were about the fidelity of his wife, my godmother, and that is because she liked to talk, she was voluble, and she dressed in those light shoulder strap dresses with their low necklines. About him, a serious person who kept his promises, a person you could trust completely, there had never been any suspicion. Very faithful, she repeated. Since he was being accused by greedy people who wanted to turn things to good account—and here she gave me an accusing look—she was going to betray a confidence; she didn't want to go into detail, but she was going to tell us what he had once said to her:

"I like you even too much, but I'll never betray my wife."

She made it clear that the two of them had never fooled around.

Finally there was a witness called by the judge, a man who must have been my age but seemed older, mainly because he was missing several teeth. He alleged that at the time I was conceived, Mama lived in Várzea Pacífica with Daddy, and my father lived with his family at the ranch, that they never saw each other.

None of these witnesses took into account the most significant fact: Raimundo's accusation that my godfather had killed Mama's husband, that is, the man I previously believed to be my father. I admit that the accusation did not formally exist and could be seen as something that Arnaldo and I had invented. The hitman had commented on the matter with us but had not appeared before the Truth Commission or left a written or recorded statement.

The lawyer then ruled that my suit was inadmissible and that I would have to pay the court fees.

The representative from the State Prosecutor's Office opined on the inadmissibility of my suit. Some of his arguments were laughable: my birth certificate had my father's name on it, not my godfather's. My godfather's will named only two children, Clarice and Miguel, and made no reference to me.

The judge, a jovial forty-year old, and certainly a friend of Miguel's, cited the Code of Civil Procedural Law in his decision stating that the onus of proof lay on the plaintiff when it came to establishing the fact of his rights. That I would have to demonstrate biological filiation, but that from analysis of the oral proofs produced, it was not evident that Mama had had any amorous liaison with my godfather. On the contrary, various witnesses had categorically denied it had happened. Although one witness had affirmed that I looked like my godfather, that had little significance, and the oral proof produced in the records was not sufficient to conclude that I was his biological son. Given the absence of expert evidence, only a coherent and clear set of probative evidence would authorize the declaration of any biological connection. It had not happened in this case. It was his duty to assume an attitude of balance, on the one hand to perform his duty to protect just claims and on the other hand to avoid being an instrument of audacious and irresponsible ventures.

He lamented the sacralization, indeed the deification of the DNA test, which was now considered to be a miraculous formula. The excessive confidence in a scientific procedure—a cultish and a blind acceptance of the authority of the DNA—had done away with classic means of proof. Such tests were fallible, errors could occur, since the labs did not have the statistical data appropriate to the Brazilian people, who had special characteristics to do with miscegenation—data which differed from the statistical reference markers of the peoples of Europe and the United States. The DNA test therefore could not be considered definitive and absolute proof. Since it was not conclusive proof and was subject to error, it would be very risky to assume paternity simply because someone refused to take the test. And it would be a paradox to sanction the defendants indirectly for their refusal, when there was no direct sanction for such a refusal.

A legal action of this type provoked emotional disturbances in those under investigation. In the absence of any clear evidence, Clarice and Miguel's indignant refusal of corporal examination or inspection was natural. It was not prudent or ethical aprioristically to coerce persons to submit to a DNA test, threatening them with a presumption that could provoke injustices. And it would also be illegal, because no law—he repeated—forced such a procedure. Nobody was obliged to do or not do something except under the law. Those under investigation, Clarice and Miguel, therefore had the right not to submit their bodies to an undesired test.

He cited the Constitution, and repeated the principle of legality—that one cannot coerce someone to practice an act that is not legally obligatory—and he added that the plaintiffs would also be guaranteed the right to decline to provide proof against themselves, in name of balance between the parties, a fundamental premise of judicial procedures. He wound up his reasoning with the principle of dignity of the human person, protection for the inviolability of intimacy and private life, including—he insisted—the untouchability of the human body, a principle without which violence would be committed in a case in which there was a clear absence of a criminal act.

The judge then spoke, in conclusion, of the principle of weighting, which in turn was based on other principles, that of reasonableness, proportionality and balance, all of them fundamental to resolving legal conflicts. Having done that, he judged my suit to be inadmissible and the deed to be extinct, with a resolution of merit, in the terms of the Civil Procedure Code, and he ordered me, as required by the defense counsel, to pay all costs and legal fees.

December 14

I can still appeal to a higher court. In face of the impossibility of demanding, as I would like, the exhumation of the remains as proof, since my godfather's ashes floated down Black Creek to one of those reservoirs and from there certainly to the overflow, to other creeks, to rivers and possibly to the Atlantic Ocean, I will have to put forward new elements of proof. But what elements, if they don't actually exist?

I know, because she told me, that Clarice kept some of her father's ashes in a can before throwing the rest in the creek. Those ashes could be analyzed. The procedure, I know in advance, is at the total discretion of the judge. Even if Miguel and Clarice agree—and I know that they will not—the judge is still not obliged to defer to my request, since it is an exceptional measure justifiable only if its need and pertinence are proven. They are obvious to me since there are no other probatory measures at my disposal and the DNA of those ashes is the essential point of the process, which would resolve all uncertainties.

Perhaps the only strategy left to me is seduction. Who knows, maybe Clarice will receive me and let me remind her how important she was and still is in my life. I will sway her with the truth: that my action has nothing to do with inheritance. And what's more, I renounce the inheritance. That, despite the conflict that has sprung up between us, I love her and want to know whether she is my sister. Face to face, I hope to convince her. If she really does not want to do the exam, at least let them examine the ashes that she has certainly kept.

Christmas is coming. I'm bad at choosing presents. Clothing sizes confuse me. I'm no good at shoes either. I know she has small feet, but does she wear a thirty-four or a thirty-six? A pretty little box, perhaps. Chocolates? That would be too little. Jewelry? I'll see if I can find a ring that is like that old one I gave her, but this time in real gold. I doubt I'll find one here, in Várzea Pacífica, where there's nothing nice to buy. There isn't even a florist in town.

December 19
I learned today of the death of the poor man who did time in prison for the murder of the man I thought was my father. I had visited him twice in the hospital, not to try to redeem my guilt or to protect myself from any police investigation but moved by pity and sincerely

wishing for his recovery. I was the only one to visit him.
In fact he was alone, as they had told me. I was thinking
of visiting him again on Christmas Day.

There would certainly be no wake, and he would be
buried as an indigent. Now that I think of it, since he's
dead, the heirs will show up. After all, he had a store.

I know I shouldn't mix sadness with happiness. But what
can I do if both come up on the same day? I remembered Mirna, my flight companion between Brasília and
Fortaleza. I don't have the slightest idea why I remembered her. I went on Facebook and found several women
with her name and I recognized her photo in one of the
profiles. I sent her a friend request, and in a matter of
seconds, she accepted. So I can end my sad day with a
little happiness.

6. Brasília

January 10

I'LL LEAVE THE DECISION about what to do about Clarice until later. I can't meet her so soon. Now I have a more important mission. Five days ago my ex-wife's elder sister called me. Patrícia may be dying. I'm not religious, but desperation led me to prayer. If there is a God, may He manifest Himself. Until now, He has not made Himself manifest. I got on a plane and went straight to Brasília.

On Christmas Day, still at Black Creek, I called Clarice's cellphone. If she'd answered, I'd have wished her a Merry Christmas. If I'd have felt welcome, I'd have paid her a visit to give her the present I bought her, the ring. She didn't pick up.

I called again on December 31 to wish her a Happy New Year. Nothing.

I spent the end of the year alone, picking mangoes from the leafy mango tree that gives shade to the front of the house, looking at the grass that was turning green with the first rains, and the hills of the neighboring properties that distance polished with gray tones and where you could see minuscule sheep at pasture. My thoughts roamed up and down those hills, entered one property after another, visited the past, the times of my childhood, until nightfall shrouded my sadness.

Not even Arnaldo showed up. On January 2, I called Clarice again, prepared for either the worst or the best. The worst: she'd hang up on me. The best: I'd listen to her apologies, imagining her on her knees at my feet, and I holding her hands firmly, helping her to stand and placing the ring on her finger.

I did not sense hate in her voice.

"I've never forgotten something you told me, I'll come back," she said into the cellphone.

I don't remember having told her that, but just as we assign special value to a sentence in a book because it tells us something special, in a conversation we also choose strong, significant words that the other says— and many times says without realizing their importance or meaning.

I preferred not to provoke Clarice with the difficult matter. The conversation opened the door that one day, who knows, would give me access to a clearer space where we could finally come to an understanding.

January 11
I was happy to leave my little ranch at Black Creek. My life had lost its meaning, despite the surprisingly good cotton harvest. The world was collapsing around me, an

impassable abyss was opening in front of me. I couldn't sleep last night. The smallest worries prolonged my insomnia. No thought or promise could relieve them. So much energy spent on small things! Then the threat of death arrives to place everything in its proper perspective and make me think that I am also what I was.

Ah, how I would like to liberate what I have repressed, to melt in tears into Patrícia's arms, to reveal my fragility, to acknowledge my mistake! But I'm not even capable of that. When I think about our fight, which was, I recognize, merely the final straw before we separated, I still want her to apologize. I know that's not going to happen, especially not now. I'm numb in the face of misfortune. Is my anguish proof of my love? Of its remains? It is proof, certainly, of the importance that Patrícia holds for me as a source of suffering. I like the idea of being near her, of helping her in her most difficult moment. Love is a struggle, a struggle for life.

A dizzying anguish casts our best years into the abyss: our honeymoon in Rio, our excursions to Caldas Novas, our camping trips to the Chapada dos Veadeiros, our days by the Itiquira waterfalls, our warm Sunday afternoons, painful memories of a good time, when she was singing in a cheap bar, a chronicle of happy imperfections.

"There is nobody in the world like you," she said one golden afternoon under the coconut trees, while the wind gently moaned its lament. I didn't know what to answer, because I thought what she said was a tawdry verse from some banal song, like the ones she sang in the wee hours of the morning, not something written especially for me.

And why do I remember this now? It's because memory charges dividends from the past. Patrícia is the best woman in the world. I should have fought for her. Unlike Clarice, who returned to Várzea Pacífica, and from what I know, retreated into her house, surrounded by few friends, Patrícia was, yes, a woman of the world. Too much of a party girl? A nightclub singer? Had she been with more men than I would have liked? In the backlands, it would not have been accepted, I know that. And what did I care if in Fortaleza everyone knew she had lost her virginity before marrying me? Her reputation, even if it's in keeping with the truth, is fictitious, a story invented by those who couldn't have her.

What mattered to me when I met Patrícia was that she had a heart that was sensitive to beauty and suffering. When I embraced and kissed her, I felt that I was possessing her entirely, including her selfless and rebellious spirit. She would throw her hair back and open up a wide, mysterious smile, her face growing, and in that moment, I was certain I needed her, as I needed the unknown things that made me suffer.

I remember the early days of our love. A week after I met Patrícia, Miguel lent me a car, a noisy blue DKW Vermag. It wasn't his, but my godfather had bought that car, which he left in Uncle's garage in Fortaleza, when Miguel turned eighteen, precisely so his son would start to drive it.

I took Patrícia to a dune at the Praia do Futuro, and

the car stalled on the gravel road, which had been invaded by the sand. A couple passing in another car along the Corrida de Submarinos, where couples would park to have car sex, stopped to help us. Patrícia sank into the seat, not wanting to be seen. Since we could not find pieces of wood, the muscular guy from the other car, who was about my age, and I laid down stones to support the tires. Finally we were able to get the car out of the rut. I drove the DKW Vermag to the highest point of the dune. It was a night of a new moon, the sky was covered with points of light, we could see all the constellations.

I talked about my plans for the future, I wanted to be a lawyer. Patrícia had a distracted look, lost in the secrets of the night that only the stars knew. I kissed her lips and held her in a long embrace.

Car headlights illuminated the road below, near the water's edge. Almost imperceptible sparkles marked the lines of the waves, which rose and fell, minuscule and soft. The immense, dark sea dominated the center of the landscape. A ship, which in the distance was as small as a toy, passed along the horizon. The wind snored its own snore at the window of the car, carrying the noise of another car that was descending the dunes. To the right and left were the arched silhouettes of the dunes.

Looking at the broad landscape, I convinced Patrícia to go to a motel near the beach, whose rectangular lights we could see. I paid in cash and parked the car in the private garage attached to the room.

No sooner had we climbed the stairs and entered the room than she threw the shoulder bag she was carrying on the bed. Then she ran her slender fingers slowly along the lines of my right palm, a gypsy telling my future. I sensed something ceremonious and tragic in the touch of her long nails, painted a light pink.

"If I decided to live with you, my family would not support me. And you don't have any money," she said.

"No, I don't," I answered truthfully, finding her comment strange.

"So . . . let's not screw this up.

"Money isn't everything in life," I answered firmly.

"I don't want to keep meeting you in secret. And you want to keep waiting for me . . ."

"Until we can get married? I'll wait as long as I have to."

Perhaps it was momentary sincerity, to which she responded, perhaps falsely, while she slung her purse over her shoulder, making a motion to leave:

"I wasn't even thinking about marriage."

"They'll think it's strange that we didn't stay for even a minute."

She grasped the doorknob and stopped to look at me:

"The problem is that we're not independent. I still depend on my parents and my elder sister. And you don't have money. I know money isn't everything, but I don't have the disposition for such an affair. I am afraid."

"You're right," I said, not making it clear whether I agreed that I didn't have money or that she was afraid.

Patrícia started to tremble and cry. She sat on the floor next to the door.

"We would have to . . ."

She didn't finish the sentence.

I took the purse off her shoulder and put her back on the bed. I leaned over her and started to embrace and kiss Patrícia as I had just done on the dunes.

"No," she pushed me with her feet, still crying.

I felt in that rejection her desire to embrace me, finally to confess that she loved me. Despite all that, she wasn't ready to go to bed with me. Her desperate look scanned the walls of the room. Then in a violent gesture, she got up, put her purse on her shoulder again, opened the door and burst out of the room, with me following her down the stairs to the garage.

I learned early on, from experience and before the television soap operas taught me, that love and suffering were a single thing. Later I read that the value of love is the sum of what you have to pay for it; that whenever you've been able to love without effort and suffering, you've been wrong.

I would meet Patrícia at the bar on the Maranguape road where she sang. In the beginning, our relationship was tumultuous. I hated going to her shows because her voice and beauty attracted the attention of many fans.

"I like only you," she assured me.

We would stay at the bar until two in the morning and then go to a coconut palm grove near Mama's store in Mondubim, in an abandoned lot.

After months of romance, she got pregnant with Pedro, our son, who today is an engineer and lives in São Paulo. I won't say that's why we got married, but I wasn't earning very much, which worried her, and if it hadn't been for the child, we would have waited longer. Confronted with a fait accompli, I thought it better that we live together, even if we were all crowded together in the room at the back of the store.

Patrícia refused at first. I had to insist. I convinced her when she was three months pregnant. We would survive, and it would be better if we were together to take care of our son.

The wedding took place in the Mondubim chapel. It was a simple ceremony, with not many people. Mama was present along with Patrícia's older sister. Since I didn't want my godmother to come, I didn't invite my godfather. Although invited, Clarice and my aunt and uncle didn't come. Miguel arrived late and stayed late. Uncle was going through financial difficulties, he told me. He was a loan shark. One of his biggest debtors had defaulted and if he demanded payment from him, he would denounce his illegal activities to the police.

January 13

The beginning of my marriage to Patrícia was not more difficult, because we were in love.

"Our honeymoon will last forever. Until death," she said to me. "Promise that only death will separate us?"

"I promise," I answered, believing what I said.

"It's all or nothing," she added. "If the marriage goes flat, it's better to end it."

· "That won't happen. True love doesn't end."

"Right. Love doesn't wither. We can wither. Then love will go."

"What an idea, don't even say that!"

Our biggest problem was money. We counted every cent. I kept part of the profits from the store, which were meagre, and Patrícia earned an occasional pittance with her shows.

"I've been invited to sing in another bar," she told me.

She would stay out later and later and have to travel farther and farther. But in return, she earned more.

I started to feel uncomfortable when she arrived at three in the morning, after hitching a ride.

"Don't you want your wife to help with the expenses? Don't you want me to work?"

"It's not that, you know it."

The bar shows didn't last. For two months, during which Patrícia couldn't find anywhere to sing, she practiced her repertoire at home, with a guitar, which she played by ear.

When she started to sing again at another bar, also until late and even on weeknights, I couldn't hide my fits of jealousy. I would come home from classes at the Law School and find her surrounded by friends. They would make caipirinhas and stay up until dawn singing to the sound of the guitar. One of those times, a photographer friend kept praising Patrícia's beauty and suggested she do a portfolio; he would help her get her photograph in the newspapers and magazines. It seemed to me that Patrícia melted when she heard his praise and I doubted that her love for me would hold up to the talk and the looks of the guy I thought was perfect, whereas I down-played my own qualities.

"Why don't you come with me to the bar?" she suggested.

I got almost no sleep when I accompanied her to the bar until the small hours, because I worked in the shop during the day, and at night I went to Law School. Sometimes when I went to bed, she would still be up. When I got up, she would sleep late. When I got home, I'd find a note from her: "I'll be home later tonight." Then she would stay out the whole night and I slept poorly. She would arrive, undress, I saw her slender, well-formed body, and then she would lie down next to me, her big eyes close to my face, she would embrace me and take off my clothes.

"I missed you," she said.

She continued her shows at the bars, on Saturdays, even after Pedro was born. I went with her, we took the baby, so he would get used to the noise and because we didn't have any other choice. During the day, seven days a week, I helped Mama at the store, Pedro at our side, our first son, today an engineer, and who at that time only laughed, cried and slept. Patrícia didn't always nurse him but when she wasn't there, she would leave her milk in a bottle and Mama or I would feed the baby. At night I would take a bus in Mondubim that went through Parangaba and Benfica and left me not far from the Praça Clóvis Beviláqua, where the Law School was located.

After toiling at temporary jobs, I was able to get work as an attorney. When we moved from Fortaleza to the

Federal District, Patrícia stopped singing. The job at the
Post Office occupied her but did not please her. To make
up for it, she sang private shows at home, entertaining
friends we invited to barbeques in the backyard of our
house in Taguatinga.

Still January 13
Patrícia is certain she hasn't got much longer to live.
I kissed her hands, without the courage to do more.
Her fragile expression was thankful, with a glimmer of
contentment.

She perhaps loved me once and still loves me, and I'm
the one who didn't understand that. In the depths of her
fading eyes, a glimmer, a distant star, reminds me of our
old passion. When we were still in love, we made three
sons. Pedro and Paulo live in São Paulo, I think I already
said that. Teodoro is the manager of the hotel where I
stayed in Fortaleza. He's about to get married. What he
calls a wedding is just a civil union. Everyone will arrive
tomorrow and maybe the two paulistas, the guys from
São Paulo, as I call them, will not want to see me.

Why remember the difficult moments that Patrícia
and I went through? One thing is certain: I'm the person closest to her as she is on the verge of death. Despite
what the doctors tell me, I agree with Patrícia; I think
she is going to die soon. I should say, on the other hand,
that nobody was as intimate with me as she was, not
even Clarice. The truth be told, compared with her
Clarice is nothing. When Patrícia dies, will I be able

to look for Clarice? No, wouldn't it be better never to see Clarice again, another Clarice, an old Clarice, a wounded Clarice because I wanted to discover and reveal the truth? Well, the old Clarice has nothing to do with the young Clarice I knew, the girl I should perhaps keep intact, the same as a childhood experience and an adolescent fantasy. What will Clarice be for me in the future? I can't ask this question without an upsurge of nervousness. And what if she is indeed my sister?

January 14

Patrícia snores like a pig. She vomits like my dying grandmother, a yellow vomit the texture of sugary paste, with streaks of green and red. Helping her like a nurse in these circumstances is an opportunity to redeem myself. I will stay by her side until the end, I've decided that. I sometimes hold her cold hands, thinking that the last moment has arrived and that, if eternity exists for her, we'll be there together holding hands. But what if she survives?

Today I cried. I cried a lot. I hid my tears from Patrícia. She and I have gone through so much together . . . I don't have to say what. It was a whole lifetime, talking every day about the few options we had, knowing we had great difficulties and facing them together in solidarity, being happy about what we did when we were in love, making our three sons, educating them . . .

They have just arrived from Fortaleza and São Paulo. Teodoro embraced me. Pedro and Paulo greeted me with averted eyes, but still they greeted me. Extreme experiences, like the threat of death, bring the living together.

February 20
I felt devastated after Patrícia's expected death. I regret not having been at the hospital on the fateful night, not having held her hands in the decisive and irreversible instant, not having, therefore, been able to prove that I would be at her side for eternity. In compensation, I gave each of my sons a prolonged hug.

The wake was held at the Campo da Esperança cemetery, in Chapel number seven. I sent a notice to Patrícia's work colleagues, the ones at the Post Office. I contacted her relatives, just the closest ones. I called my few friends. My sons thought it was appropriate to call some of their friends, people I saw there for the first time. Several wreaths arrived, some with messages from people I don't know, perhaps old fans of Patrícia's.

After returning from the cemetery, I stayed here drinking beer; I've already had three, which haven't helped me overcome my sadness at all. I want to forget Black Creek and Várzea Pacífica. I came back from the cemetery thinking that Várzea Pacífica is not the same any more, just as the people I knew are no longer the same. There are cities that don't change, they don't get old or modernize, but those are far away, perhaps in Europe. Here they change quickly like cloud formations or the moods of social media.

The crimes in Várzea Pacífica are no longer the

same. In the old days they happened among enemies or ex-friends, even among neighbors, people who knew each other and got together in bars or at parties, who saw each other in the city streets; they were crimes that happened because of jealousy, pride, spite, honor, or ambition. Today there are many muggings, and more hidden crimes. Certainly the great construction projects, the dam, the bridge, and the asphalt road, which is already full of potholes, must have paid off more than what was owed to the contractors who contributed to the mayoral campaigns.

While I was there, I went to the cemetery—very different from this one in Brasília, because it has tombs with cement constructions and sinuous paths. I wanted to visit Grandma, to prostate myself before her tomb, which was simpler than most. How can I erase the suffering she felt because I abandoned her? To this day, Grandma is present in my life. Every time I drink my beers, like now, I remember her. Grandma never liked it when you drank. But one day, she discovered the cachaça, which she mixed with water. If it weren't ridiculous, I would wear a pair of black Nycron pants and put a black handkerchief in the pocket of my white shirt, like when Grandma died.

The realization of Patrícia's death stays with me, it does not abandon me, not just because she died a short time ago; perhaps it will never leave me. When a mere landscape or a glimpse of the future brings me a touch of happiness, I feel guilty. I am in mourning. Truly in mourning. In perpetual mourning. I close my eyes to the world and rediscover my sadness at Patrícia's side.

Patrícia's memory messes up my attention and my interests, ruining what I used to consider attractive. I can't even sleep. I prefer to stay here, writing, biting my nails and drinking one beer after another, when I'm not pacing around the house for hours at a time, tidying up what doesn't need tidying.

A window moans in the wind. Let it. I don't have the energy to close it. Enough for today. I won't write another line. I'm drunk.

7. Taguatinga, Sector B North, QNB 8

July 4

I WAS ABLE TO rent out the Taguatinga house, which brings back sad memories of Patrícia, and I moved to this one in Sector B North, in QNB 8, which is also in Taguatinga.

Most importantly, I gave up the idea of returning to Black Creek. I've permanently swapped the ranch for the city. I prefer the hum of cars, the overflowing gutters, the traffic jams, the featureless city blocks, the solitude in the company of millions of others. They say that Brasília is horrible, and Taguatinga is worse. What do I care, if this is where I made my life? They can say what they want, I like this strange place, which is mine, in this dry season colored by the Ipê trees.

Luzia wrote me at Christmas almost two months after Patrícia's death. I didn't expect anything from her. She said she had received the news late, she was very sad and hoped I would find the strength to cope with my terrible loss. I don't know if she knew I was separated from

Patrícia.

Clarice and Miguel didn't send their condolences. There are people like that, whose silence torments you; they are present through their absence.

August 14

Noteworthy since Patrícia's death is that a few days ago I went to Teodoro's wedding in Fortaleza. He married the nice guy he had introduced me to. I think they have a lot in common and have a sincere affection for each other, which as I've already said, will double their moments of happiness and reduce their sadness in moments of sadness by half. The party was simple, in a beach house at Praia da Taíba, lent by a friend, and attended by their closest acquaintances. It was a symbolic act, and symbols endure, they defy time. I'm beginning to get along with Teodoro. I don't know if I can say the same thing for Pedro and Paulo, who didn't even come to their brother's wedding. I think they disapprove of it.

I took advantage of being in Fortaleza to call Mirna, the girl I had met a year and a half ago on the Brasília-Fortaleza flight and who reminded me of Luzia. To my surprise she didn't ignore my call and even accepted my invitation to dinner at one of the beach restaurants at the Praia do Futuro. I put the ring that I had bought for Clarice in my pocket. Who knows, it might bring good luck.

After some coconut water and snacks at the bar, I

suggested we walk on the beach. We took off our shoes and walked barefoot, sinking our feet in the sand, kicking the bubbling water that the waves brought and feeling the salty fresh breeze on our faces. We talked about almost everything, or rather about what I do, what she does, what I like to do, what she likes to do, what I've stopped doing and what she has too, and we agreed the world is in bad shape but better than when there was a high mortality rate, when there was no penicillin or even a fraction of the medical resources available today, that Brazil is a mess, but the same mess as always, with its ups and downs, a disaster with more violence and less illiterate people. She wanted to know about my time at university, about the cases I've defended, about what it was like to live in Taguatinga, about my plans . . .

"Oh, how cool," she repeated after every story I told.

When we returned to the restaurant, I said:

"Thank you for going out with me," and I quickly regretted the awkward statement.

She looked at me curiously, as if she were studying me, and finally could read my thoughts. I thought that in that look there was an embryo of desire. Soon, however, her gaze shifted to the sea, became indifferent. After we had sat down at the table, she looked me in the eye and laughed. Would that be the moment to take the conversation to intimate territory, I thought. Mirna anticipated my thought saying:

"Do you know I'm getting married?"

Even with this she reminded me of Luzia, who had come looking for me on the eve of her wedding.

"With a friend, who is also a professor."

They had known each other a long time, but their romance was recent. He had taken the initiative. She hesitated at first, and then came to the conclusion that he was the person she liked the most, although she had never thought he could be her husband or even her boyfriend. Was it a mistake to accept his proposal? Of course not, I answered, calming her the way I had done when there was turbulence on the Brasília-Fortaleza flight.

I was pleased she was about to get married and again I thought of Luzia. If she was already committed, it would be less complicated to sleep with her, a transitory act with no strings attached. It would exempt us from future commitments.

On the other hand, looking into Mirna's face, I noticed an expression of sobriety and respect for me that left me reluctant to make an unserious proposal. I would not succeed, because, to begin with, I wasn't sure about what to do.

It was then that I was unexpectedly overcome with a sentiment of affection, one which was also physical; I could feel it in my blood. If I'd had white skin, certainly at that moment my face would have been completely red. Mirna appeared to be more attractive than ever, but not for an affair. Logically and rationally, I knew I shouldn't move into a territory as dangerous as love. But I was feeling emotional and I let the emotion guide me to tell Mirna I didn't know what, perhaps that I would be capable of loving her, or more daringly, that I loved her. An idea flew through my head, a little loosely and suddenly:

a new marriage. I felt a trembling inside me. Was I really in love? Should I be sincere and say what I was feeling? It could be something very fleeting and besides that, I didn't know women anymore, they were different. My sincerity could blow everything. What should I say first?

"Do you believe in love?" I asked.

"Do you?"

"I think I've only loved two women in my life and I desired another one deeply," I said with words that came to me unplanned, but they were correct and necessary.

"Tell me everything."

I continued, sincerely, I think because I was still crushed by what had recently happened to me. I told her about Clarice and about Patrícia. I didn't talk about Luzia, whom she reminded me of and who in fact had drawn me to her. Paying attention to every detail, she listened, looking at me intently, furrowing her brow, and twice patting my hands affectionately.

Over dinner we strayed from the heavy subject. We talked about banalities. She promised to introduce me to her future husband, and we agreed to see each other when I passed through Fortaleza again. She said I should send her an e-mail or call, or if I preferred, we could use WhatsApp.

I think she likes me, even admires me. But she treats me like an old man, perhaps someone who reminds her of her grandfather. Isn't she right? I felt as superficial as Luzia was on the eve of her wedding, shameless for calling Mirna, but who knows I might go to her wedding if she invites me.

I'll keep the ring for now, and if I can't find a better purpose for it, one day I'll sell it.

August 27
I don't want to see Clarice again, or even talk to her on the phone. She didn't bother to call when Patrícia died. If she calls, I'll hang up on her. If she writes on Facebook or sends an e-mail, I won't answer. I don't want anything more to do with Black Creek or Várzea Pacífica, unless it's to revive my paternity investigation. For that I still need to regain my strength.

For now the goal is to sell that devil of a ranch and pay off my debts. Arnaldo says he's taking care of it, he'll find a buyer. I promised him a commission, which he refused. I want him to come and visit me. He liked the idea. He's never left that place; he's never even been to Fortaleza. And hopefully, despite everything, there'll be another good cotton harvest!

Memory is treacherous. It does not preserve the past, it doesn't bring back what was lost. What remains of the Black Creek Ranch, of Várzea Pacífica, are poor allusions to what they were to me. What remains of the Clarice I knew is garbage; I don't know or want to know. The past is dead, as I said, and if I didn't, I'll say it now to whomever wants to listen. Dead forever? I didn't know until now. It's sad, but true, it's dead forever. I look inside myself: my spirit has dried up, like the landscape of the backlands at the height of summer. I feel destroyed, like my red brick house.

September 10
I saw Clarice's phone number appear on my cell phone screen. What could she still want with me? I hesitated for a second before I decided to answer the call. I heard her claim that I shouldn't take into account the babbling of a bandit who concocted a statement in front of a Commission whose conclusions were not legally binding; that my godfather would never have hired a hitman. Absurd! Lousy bandit. Scoundrel. Liar. And I was an idiot for believing it, she accused me. I almost hit the button to disconnect the call.

"I'm not going to discuss this over the phone," I answered, without understanding why she had called to repeat using different words the same thing she spat in my face all that time ago.

Then she revealed that Miguel was interested in buying my property, that they'd found out from Arnaldo that it was for sale. Miguel has a fondness for the land, the big house; they bring back good memories.

"Why is he showing interest in that land now? Why didn't he buy it before?" I asked.

"Call him. Despite everything, he likes you."

I thought of what Patrícia had said on the day of the huge fight that led to our separation and then I asked Clarice:

"And you, why don't you buy it? Doesn't it bring you back good memories?"

"No, I'm not sentimental."

I heard a long, uncomfortable silence.

"Are you my sister?"

"Think of me as if I were. I'm your sister, there. And stop being a pain in the ass. I'm not doing any tests," she said, telling me what I already knew, albeit with less anger than I expected.

"I don't accept that answer."

"So don't accept it. I like you, guy. I like you as a sister."

"You know we're more than just brother and sister."

"I don't know what you mean by that. It would be best if we ended this conversation."

"Look here, Clarice. If you want to be straight with me, call back. I won't call you again."

"Well, 'bye then."

21 September

I wasn't going to call Miguel, but I answered an e-mail from him two days after Clarice's call. I'm old, and old age softens your heart. I agreed to take his call. After all, despite the the factories going bust, I imagined he'd still have the money to buy the land. Why not sell it to someone I knew? There was a lot to discuss, but I didn't feel comfortable discussing sensitive topics such as murder over the phone.

This time he didn't ask after Zuleide. We talked about business, although his hesitations, the tone of his voice, and his silences in particular indicated a desire to touch on other subjects, since silences can contain memories, pain, despair, forgiveness, as well as hurt and hate. A point of pride prevented me from telling Miguel that I still felt affection for him. I forgave him inside, but there is no pardon without traces of suffering, or a reunion without the memory of a separation. I imagined fighting with him on a dune in Tibau, exchanging imaginary gunfire, defeating him, the two of us grappling on the sand, and we finally agreed on a price somewhere in the middle.

We are brothers who were born unequal, one poor, another rich. We took different paths in life. The more time has passed, the more our differences have deepened, but even so we perceive—at least this is what I think—that we are blood of the same blood and we are capable of creating—not now, but who knows, one day?—spaces for dialogue and reconciliation.

I know it was chance that took me away from the backlands, back then and now once again, and that the past does not ask permission to return as a memory. The past will continue there, as in a prison, sometimes freeing itself to torment me on sleepless nights. The dead, I think I said, live in the living, and Patrícia, Clarice and Luzia—who have also died, because they are from another time—will always live within me, forever young, each in her own way.

Why evoke the past? Sometimes it hides in objects that never return to our experience. At other times, chance brings back a lived emotion, and the illusion prompts us to travel and gives us the impression that we are reliving it again. Nevertheless, I must admit, it does not substitute the present, the inherent difficulties of the unknown or the uncertain promises of the future.

Translator's Note

TRANSLATING NOVELS OF the Brazilian Northeast into English presents specific challenges, including tone, register, sociolect, and lexis, particularly the terminology of the place names, geography, flora and fauna of the region. The tone and register fluctuate in this novel between the interior monologue of the narrator, the words he sets on the page (with the disclaimer that he is writing "quickly and without regard for style or vocabulary"), and the dialogues he records with family members, friends, and acquaintances from the past and the present. The narrator has evolved from his position as a young, illiterate (in his words, "subaltern") boy, son of a black woman who lives and works on the ranch owned by his godfather, to a successful lawyer practicing in Brasília. When the narrator recalls episodes and dialogues of his past, he reproduces the speech patterns, cadences and grammatical features of the language spoken by those who live in the remote backlands. It is a spoken language with roots in medieval Portuguese, and exhibits archaic verb forms, in particular the use of the informal "tu" with the third person verb form. The register shifts back to modern, urban Brazilian Portuguese in the dialogues with characters from the narrator's present. While difficult to make this beautiful northeastern speech sing in English, I have attempted to capture its cadence and rhythm. It is impossible to evoke the sounds and smells of the northeast backlands in words only; olfactory and auditory memory place a part in rendering these sensual experiences, and I can only hope I have done it partial justice through my own memories of the region. Place names and the names of streets have been kept in the original, as is standard practice.

Another distinctive feature of this novel consists of the constant shifts in time, consistent with the theme of memory in the novel. These shifts can be seen as a kind of montage or collage effect that is similar to the techniques of film narrative. The use of different forms of past tense (more complex in Portuguese than English) from imperfect, to simple past, to past preterite, conditional preterite, to past subjunctive, create a blurring effect that corresponds to the very instability of memory that the author articulates in his narrative. In this way, Almino creates a text that challenges the mode of assembling the narrative. By creating a deliberately ambiguous text, João Almino, like his Portuguese counterpart Antonio Lobo Antunes, puts narrative reliability in question by presenting it as a kind of lie by which the narrator seeks impossible salvation or, at least, shelter from a potentially damning present.

I thank the author, João Almino, for his careful reading of my translation and his helpful suggestions. My
thanks and appreciation to John O'Brien, publisher of
Dalkey Archive Press, for his confidence in me, and for
his vision and persistence in bringing great works of
world literature to the English-language audience.

Elizabeth Lowe

MICHAL AJVAZ, *The Golden Age.*
The Other City.
PIERRE ALBERT-BIROT, *Grabinoulor.*
YUZ ALESHKOVSKY, *Kangaroo.*
FELIPE ALFAU, *Chromos.*
Locos.
JOE AMATO, *Samuel Taylor's Last Night.*
IVAN ÂNGELO, *The Celebration.*
The Tower of Glass.
ANTÓNIO LOBO ANTUNES, *Knowledge of Hell.*
The Splendor of Portugal.
ALAIN ARIAS-MISSON, *Theatre of Incest.*
JOHN ASHBERY & JAMES SCHUYLER, *A Nest of Ninnies.*
ROBERT ASHLEY, *Perfect Lives.*
GABRIELA AVIGUR-ROTEM, *Heatwave and Crazy Birds.*
DJUNA BARNES, *Ladies Almanack.*
Ryder.
JOHN BARTH, *Letters.*
Sabbatical.
DONALD BARTHELME, *The King.*
Paradise.
SVETISLAV BASARA, *Chinese Letter.*
MIQUEL BAUÇÀ, *The Siege in the Room.*
RENÉ BELLETTO, *Dying.*
MAREK BIENCZYK, *Transparency.*
ANDREI BITOV, *Pushkin House.*
ANDREJ BLATNIK, *You Do Understand.*
Law of Desire.
LOUIS PAUL BOON, *Chapel Road.*
My Little War.
Summer in Termuren.
ROGER BOYLAN, *Killoyle.*
IGNÁCIO DE LOYOLA BRANDÃO, *Anonymous Celebrity.*
Zero.
BONNIE BREMSER, *Troia: Mexican Memoirs.*
CHRISTINE BROOKE-ROSE, *Amalgamemnon.*
BRIGID BROPHY, *In Transit.*
The Prancing Novelist.

GERALD L. BRUNS, *Modern Poetry and the Idea of Language.*
GABRIELLE BURTON, *Heartbreak Hotel.*
MICHEL BUTOR, *Degrees.*
Mobile.
G. CABRERA INFANTE, *Infante's Inferno.*
Three Trapped Tigers.
JULIETA CAMPOS, *The Fear of Losing Eurydice.*
ANNE CARSON, *Eros the Bittersweet.*
ORLY CASTEL-BLOOM, *Dolly City.*
LOUIS-FERDINAND CÉLINE, *North.*
Conversations with Professor Y.
London Bridge.
MARIE CHAIX, *The Laurels of Lake Constance.*
HUGO CHARTERIS, *The Tide Is Right.*
ERIC CHEVILLARD, *Demolishing Nisard.*
The Author and Me.
MARC CHOLODENKO, *Mordechai Schamz.*
JOSHUA COHEN, *Witz.*
EMILY HOLMES COLEMAN, *The Shutter of Snow.*
ERIC CHEVILLARD, *The Author and Me.*
ROBERT COOVER, *A Night at the Movies.*
STANLEY CRAWFORD, *Log of the S.S. The Mrs Unguentine.*
Some Instructions to My Wife.
RENÉ CREVEL, *Putting My Foot in It.*
RALPH CUSACK, *Cadenza.*
NICHOLAS DELBANCO, *Sherbrookes.*
The Count of Concord.
NIGEL DENNIS, *Cards of Identity.*
PETER DIMOCK, *A Short Rhetoric for Leaving the Family.*
ARIEL DORFMAN, *Konfidenz.*
COLEMAN DOWELL, *Island People.*
Too Much Flesh and Jabez.
ARKADII DRAGOMOSHCHENKO, *Dust.*
RIKKI DUCORNET, *Phosphor in Dreamland.*
The Complete Butcher's Tales.

FOR A FULL LIST OF PUBLICATIONS, VISIT: www.dalkeyarchive.com

RIKKI DUCORNET (cont.), *The Jade Cabinet*.
The Fountains of Neptune.

WILLIAM EASTLAKE, *The Bamboo Bed*.
Castle Keep.
Lyric of the Circle Heart.

JEAN ECHENOZ, *Chopin's Move*.

STANLEY ELKIN, *A Bad Man*.
Criers and Kibitzers, Kibitzers and Criers.
The Dick Gibson Show.
The Franchiser.
The Living End.
Mrs. Ted Bliss.

FRANÇOIS EMMANUEL, *Invitation to a Voyage*.

PAUL EMOND, *The Dance of a Sham*.

SALVADOR ESPRIU, *Ariadne in the Grotesque Labyrinth*.

LESLIE A. FIEDLER, *Love and Death in the American Novel*.

JUAN FILLOY, *Op Oloop*.

ANDY FITCH, *Pop Poetics*.

GUSTAVE FLAUBERT, *Bouvard and Pécuchet*.

KASS FLEISHER, *Talking out of School*.

JON FOSSE, *Aliss at the Fire*.
Melancholy.

FORD MADOX FORD, *The March of Literature*.

MAX FRISCH, *I'm Not Stiller*.
Man in the Holocene.

CARLOS FUENTES, *Christopher Unborn*.
Distant Relations.
Terra Nostra.
Where the Air Is Clear.

TAKEHIKO FUKUNAGA, *Flowers of Grass*.

WILLIAM GADDIS, JR., *The Recognitions*.

JANICE GALLOWAY, *Foreign Parts*.
The Trick Is to Keep Breathing.

WILLIAM H. GASS, *Life Sentences*.
The Tunnel.
The World Within the Word.
Willie Masters' Lonesome Wife.

GÉRARD GAVARRY, *Hoppla! 1 2 3*.

ETIENNE GILSON, *The Arts of the Beautiful*.
Forms and Substances in the Arts.

C. S. GISCOMBE, *Giscome Road*.
Here.

DOUGLAS GLOVER, *Bad News of the Heart*.

WITOLD GOMBROWICZ, *A Kind of Testament*.

PAULO EMÍLIO SALES GOMES, *P's Three Women*.

GEORGI GOSPODINOV, *Natural Novel*.

JUAN GOYTISOLO, *Count Julian*.
Juan the Landless.
Makbara.
Marks of Identity.

HENRY GREEN, *Blindness*.
Concluding.
Doting.
Nothing.

JACK GREEN, *Fire the Bastards!*

JIŘÍ GRUŠA, *The Questionnaire*.

MELA HARTWIG, *Am I a Redundant Human Being?*

JOHN HAWKES, *The Passion Artist*.
Whistlejacket.

ELIZABETH HEIGHWAY, ED., *Contemporary Georgian Fiction*.

AIDAN HIGGINS, *Balcony of Europe*.
Blind Man's Bluff.
Bornholm Night-Ferry.
Langrishe, Go Down.
Scenes from a Receding Past.

KEIZO HINO, *Isle of Dreams*.

KAZUSHI HOSAKA, *Plainsong*.

ALDOUS HUXLEY, *Antic Hay*.
Point Counter Point.
Those Barren Leaves.
Time Must Have a Stop.

NAOYUKI II, *The Shadow of a Blue Cat*.

DRAGO JANČAR, *The Tree with No Name*.

MIKHEIL JAVAKHISHVILI, *Kvachi*.

GERT JONKE, *The Distant Sound*.
Homage to Czerny.
The System of Vienna.

JACQUES JOUET, *Mountain R.*
Savage.
Upstaged.
MIEKO KANAI, *The Word Book.*
YORAM KANIUK, *Life on Sandpaper.*
ZURAB KARUMIDZE, *Dagny.*
JOHN KELLY, *From Out of the City.*
HUGH KENNER, *Flaubert, Joyce and Beckett: The Stoic Comedians.*
Joyce's Voices.
DANILO KIŠ, *The Attic.*
The Lute and the Scars.
Psalm 44.
A Tomb for Boris Davidovich.
ANITA KONKKA, *A Fool's Paradise.*
GEORGE KONRÁD, *The City Builder.*
TADEUSZ KONWICKI, *A Minor Apocalypse.*
The Polish Complex.
ANNA KORDZAIA-SAMADASHVILI, *Me, Margarita.*
MENIS KOUMANDAREAS, *Koula.*
ELAINE KRAF, *The Princess of 72nd Street.*
JIM KRUSOE, *Iceland.*
AYSE KULIN, *Farewell: A Mansion in Occupied Istanbul.*
EMILIO LASCANO TEGUI, *On Elegance While Sleeping.*
ERIC LAURRENT, *Do Not Touch.*
VIOLETTE LEDUC, *La Bâtarde.*
EDOUARD LEVÉ, *Autoportrait.*
Newspaper.
Suicide.
Works.
MARIO LEVI, *Istanbul Was a Fairy Tale.*
DEBORAH LEVY, *Billy and Girl.*
JOSÉ LEZAMA LIMA, *Paradiso.*
ROSA LIKSOM, *Dark Paradise.*
OSMAN LINS, *Avalovara.*
The Queen of the Prisons of Greece.
FLORIAN LIPUŠ, *The Errors of Young Tjaž.*
GORDON LISH, *Peru.*
ALF MACLOCHLAINN, *Out of Focus.*
Past Habitual.

The Corpus in the Library.
RON LOEWINSOHN, *Magnetic Field(s).*
YURI LOTMAN, *Non-Memoirs.*
D. KEITH MANO, *Take Five.*
MINA LOY, *Stories and Essays of Mina Loy.*
MICHELINE AHARONIAN MARCOM, *A Brief History of Yes.*
The Mirror in the Well.
BEN MARCUS, *The Age of Wire and String.*
WALLACE MARKFIELD, *Teitlebaum's Window.*
DAVID MARKSON, *Reader's Block.*
Wittgenstein's Mistress.
CAROLE MASO, *AVA.*
HISAKI MATSUURA, *Triangle.*
LADISLAV MATEJKA & KRYSTYNA POMORSKA, EDS., *Readings in Russian Poetics: Formalist & Structuralist Views.*
HARRY MATHEWS, *Cigarettes.*
The Conversions.
The Human Country.
The Journalist.
My Life in CIA.
Singular Pleasures.
The Sinking of the Odradek.
Stadium.
Tlooth.
HISAKI MATSUURA, *Triangle.*
DONAL MCLAUGHLIN, *beheading the virgin mary, and other stories.*
JOSEPH MCELROY, *Night Soul and Other Stories.*
ABDELWAHAB MEDDEB, *Talismano.*
GERHARD MEIER, *Isle of the Dead.*
HERMAN MELVILLE, *The Confidence-Man.*
AMANDA MICHALOPOULOU, *I'd Like.*
STEVEN MILLHAUSER, *The Barnum Museum.*
In the Penny Arcade.
RALPH J. MILLS, JR., *Essays on Poetry.*
MOMUS, *The Book of Jokes.*
CHRISTINE MONTALBETTI, *The Origin of Man.*
Western.

NICHOLAS MOSLEY, *Accident.*
Assassins.
Catastrophe Practice.
A Garden of Trees.
Hopeful Monsters.
Imago Bird.
Inventing God.
Look at the Dark.
Metamorphosis.
Natalie Natalia.
Serpent.

WARREN MOTTE, *Fables of the Novel:*
French Fiction since 1990.
Fiction Now: The French Novel in the
21st Century.
Mirror Gazing.
Oulipo: A Primer of Potential Literature.

GERALD MURNANE, *Barley Patch.*
Inland.

YVES NAVARRE, *Our Share of Time.*
Sweet Tooth.

DOROTHY NELSON, *In Night's City.*
Tar and Feathers.

ESHKOL NEVO, *Homesick.*

WILFRIDO D. NOLLEDO, *But for*
the Lovers.

BORIS A. NOVAK, *The Master of*
Insomnia.

FLANN O'BRIEN, *At Swim-Two-Birds.*
The Best of Myles.
The Dalkey Archive.
The Hard Life.
The Poor Mouth.
The Third Policeman.

CLAUDE OLLIER, *The Mise-en-Scène.*
Wert and the Life Without End.

PATRIK OUŘEDNÍK, *Europeana.*
The Opportune Moment, 1855.

BORIS PAHOR, *Necropolis.*

FERNANDO DEL PASO, *News from*
the Empire.
Palinuro of Mexico.

ROBERT PINGET, *The Inquisitory.*
Mahu or The Material.
Trio.

MANUEL PUIG, *Betrayed by Rita*
Hayworth.

The Buenos Aires Affair.
Heartbreak Tango.

RAYMOND QUENEAU, *The Last Days.*
Odile.
Pierrot Mon Ami.
Saint Glinglin.

ANN QUIN, *Berg.*
Passages.
Three.
Tripticks.

ISHMAEL REED, *The Free-Lance*
Pallbearers.
The Last Days of Louisiana Red.
Ishmael Reed: The Plays.
Juice!
The Terrible Threes.
The Terrible Twos.
Yellow Back Radio Broke-Down.

JASIA REICHARDT, *15 Journeys Warsaw*
to London.

JOÃO UBALDO RIBEIRO, *House of the*
Fortunate Buddhas.

JEAN RICARDOU, *Place Names.*

RAINER MARIA RILKE,
The Notebooks of Malte Laurids Brigge.

JULIÁN RÍOS, *The House of Ulysses.*
Larva: A Midsummer Night's Babel.
Poundemonium.

ALAIN ROBBE-GRILLET, *Project for a*
Revolution in New York.
A Sentimental Novel.

AUGUSTO ROA BASTOS, *I the Supreme.*

DANIËL ROBBERECHTS, *Arriving in*
Avignon.

JEAN ROLIN, *The Explosion of the*
Radiator Hose.

OLIVIER ROLIN, *Hotel Crystal.*

ALIX CLEO ROUBAUD, *Alix's Journal.*

JACQUES ROUBAUD, *The Form of*
a City Changes Faster, Alas, Than the
Human Heart.
The Great Fire of London.
Hortense in Exile.
Hortense Is Abducted.
Mathematics: The Plurality of Worlds of
Lewis.
Some Thing Black.

FOR A FULL LIST OF PUBLICATIONS, VISIT: www.dalkeyarchive.com

RAYMOND ROUSSEL, *Impressions of Africa.*

VEDRANA RUDAN, *Night.*

PABLO M. RUIZ, *Four Cold Chapters on the Possibility of Literature.*

GERMAN SADULAEV, *The Maya Pill.*

TOMAŽ ŠALAMUN, *Soy Realidad.*

LYDIE SALVAYRE, *The Company of Ghosts.*
The Lecture.
The Power of Flies.

LUIS RAFAEL SÁNCHEZ, *Macho Camacho's Beat.*

SEVERO SARDUY, *Cobra & Maitreya.*

NATHALIE SARRAUTE, *Do You Hear Them?*
Martereau.
The Planetarium.

STIG SÆTERBAKKEN, *Siamese.*
Self-Control.
Through the Night.

ARNO SCHMIDT, *Collected Novellas.*
Collected Stories.
Nobodaddy's Children.
Two Novels.

ASAF SCHURR, *Motti.*

GAIL SCOTT, *My Paris.*

DAMION SEARLS, *What We Were Doing and Where We Were Going.*

JUNE AKERS SEESE,
Is This What Other Women Feel Too?

BERNARD SHARE, *Inish.*
Transit.

VIKTOR SHKLOVSKY, *Bowstring.*
Literature and Cinematography.
Theory of Prose.
Third Factory.
Zoo, or Letters Not about Love.

PIERRE SINIAC, *The Collaborators.*

KJERSTI A. SKOMSVOLD,
The Faster I Walk, the Smaller I Am.

JOSEF ŠKVORECKÝ, *The Engineer of Human Souls.*

GILBERT SORRENTINO, *Aberration of Starlight.*
Blue Pastoral.
Crystal Vision.

Imaginative Qualities of Actual Things.
Mulligan Stew. Red the Fiend.
Steelwork.
Under the Shadow.

MARKO SOSIČ, *Ballerina, Ballerina.*

ANDRZEJ STASIUK, *Dukla.*
Fado.

GERTRUDE STEIN, *The Making of Americans.*
A Novel of Thank You.

LARS SVENDSEN, *A Philosophy of Evil.*

PIOTR SZEWC, *Annihilation.*

GONÇALO M. TAVARES, *A Man: Klaus Klump.*
Jerusalem.
Learning to Pray in the Age of Technique.

LUCIAN DAN TEODOROVICI,
Our Circus Presents...

NIKANOR TERATOLOGEN, *Assisted Living.*

STEFAN THEMERSON, *Hobson's Island.*
The Mystery of the Sardine.
Tom Harris.

TAEKO TOMIOKA, *Building Waves.*

JOHN TOOMEY, *Sleepwalker.*

DUMITRU TSEPENEAG, *Hotel Europa.*
The Necessary Marriage.
Pigeon Post.
Vain Art of the Fugue.

ESTHER TUSQUETS, *Stranded.*

DUBRAVKA UGRESIC, *Lend Me Your Character.*
Thank You for Not Reading.

TOR ULVEN, *Replacement.*

MATI UNT, *Brecht at Night.*
Diary of a Blood Donor.
Things in the Night.

ÁLVARO URIBE & OLIVIA SEARS, EDS.,
Best of Contemporary Mexican Fiction.

ELOY URROZ, *Friction.*
The Obstacles.

LUISA VALENZUELA, *Dark Desires and the Others.*
He Who Searches.

PAUL VERHAEGHEN, *Omega Minor.*

BORIS VIAN, *Heartsnatcher.*

LLORENÇ VILLALONGA, *The Dolls' Room.*

TOOMAS VINT, *An Unending Landscape.*

ORNELA VORPSI, *The Country Where No One Ever Dies.*

AUSTRYN WAINHOUSE, *Hedyphagetica.*

CURTIS WHITE, *America's Magic Mountain.*
The Idea of Home.
Memories of My Father Watching TV.
Requiem.

DIANE WILLIAMS,
Excitability: Selected Stories.
Romancer Erector.

DOUGLAS WOOLF, *Wall to Wall.*
Ya! & John-Juan.

JAY WRIGHT, *Polynomials and Pollen.*
The Presentable Art of Reading Absence.

PHILIP WYLIE, *Generation of Vipers.*

MARGUERITE YOUNG, *Angel in the Forest.*
Miss MacIntosh, My Darling.

REYOUNG, *Unbabbling.*

VLADO ŽABOT, *The Succubus.*

ZORAN ŽIVKOVIĆ , *Hidden Camera.*

LOUIS ZUKOFSKY, *Collected Fiction.*

VITOMIL ZUPAN, *Minuet for Guitar.*

SCOTT ZWIREN, *God Head.*

AND MORE . . .